PAPARAZZI

A NOVEL BY

MISS KP

Life Changing Books in conjunction with Power Play Media
Published by Life Changing Books
P.O. Box 423 Brandywine, MD 20613

Library of Congress Cataloging-in-Publication Data;

www.lifechangingbooks.net
13 Digit: 978-1934230398
10 Digit: 1-934230391

Follow us on Twitter: www.twitter.com/lcbooks

DEDICATION

To my better half, my soul mate, my best friend, Rodney.

ACKNOWLEDGEMENTS

I would like to begin by thanking God for blessing me with a gift that I can share with the world. This dream began with wanting to be heard and being able to touch people through literature. You have given me a gift that I have been able to share with the world and show all women that dreams do come true. If you believe in yourself the sky is the limit. To watch the transformation of women that have entered my life through this journey has been an honor, and again and I'm thankful to be blessed.

I have been blessed with a family that understands the true meaning of love.

To my husband, my soulmate, Rodney. The day I met you at Dream was the day my life changed. You showed me that love was real and to you, I'm grateful. You are a great father and I appreciate all that you do.

To my daughter, Kameron you changed my life. You will forever be my princess and I look forward to you growing up to be a God-fearing young woman. I pray that you grow up to be better than me. I will continue to cherish our close relationship. I am always here, as your protector and your guide. I love you dearly. To my son, Mateo. You are my prince that keeps me busy. I love you and now see the meaning of a mother's and son's special bond. To my son, Rodney "RNT3"and daughter, Jordan, I love you both; you make me proud to be your mom. The NBA and runway better watch out

To my mother, Lita Gray, I love you and am thankful that you taught me to work hard for what I want out of life. You did good and I'm thankful that you raised us to be a close knit family. To my father, Willis Poole, I love you and will always remain daddy's little girl. EB, thanks for being a great grandpa, love you! To my siblings, Jawaun, Mia (Brent), Cornell, and Harold (Helen). I'm thankful that I have such amazing sisters and brothers and wish you nothing but blessings. I love you all. To my nieces and nephew, Sydni, Javone, and Kyndall, I love you guys! To my Goddaughter, Ashley, I love you so much and wish only the best for you and your future!

Mema and Pop-Pop thanks for being such amazing grandparents! Eve and Jaron, you are amazing to the kids and I thank you. Delonte, Darb, Praya, and Pam thank you for being the best god-parents to my children. Alton, Dmitri, Wayne, Leon, Alan, Candace, Krystal, Kiana, Akilah, Ava, Danielle, Tat, Uncle Mark, Uncle Alan, Aunt Del (Maurice), and Uncle Rudy, love you all. To my mini West Clan, my babies Christopher, Quintez, Trey, and Arin. To Kristine West, I love you girl! Thanks for always believing me and supporting my project. From the cover to the music we are a team! Good luck with your lip gloss line, so happy for you.

Books and Babes, love you guys- Tori, Ivornette, LaFondra, Lil LaFondra, Dionne, Tonia, Nicky, and Tiesha. Thanks for your continuous support cousins!

True friends are hard to come by. Thanks to Toni, Toyia, Sharawn (Poo), Tiffany, Shana, Peta Gaye, Detrick & Renee, Gill, Rob, Donovan, Frank, Travina, Trina, Latrease, Carla CB, Karla P., Mike W., Indiah, Jermaine, Angie & Ty, Sam & Rob.

My Mt Pleasant Fam-Julette, Kiana, Deon, Ranata, Shelvy, Tarrese, Rachelle, Snookie, Janell, Pam, Shawanna, Rayshawn, Kenyatta, Joe B, Jodie, Tarik, Bernard, Demi, Donnie, Perry, and Terrance. Love my Uptown family—14th St and 640.

Many prayers to Whitey, Marcus, Woozie, KM, Gerald, Musa, and Troy P.

To the promoters that make my city the great party town

it is-Terrence Brooks, Taz & Frank Suite 202, Dee and Mike Walker of Pure Lounge, Vann and Dominique Moxcey. NYC Suave and Philly Dorian, Troy, and Tarik, thanks for great times! XQuiz thanks for your producing expertise.

Many thanks to Deb and Slantress Magazine, Jackie Hicks, Erica Wilson, Tameka Newhouse, Chris Hicks, Ella Curry, and MackMama, thanks for your support. To all the book clubs and book stores that support Urban Fiction you are greatly appreciated and make this dream come true for a lot of writers.

To my LCB family, we are truly a force to be reckoned with. To my publisher Azarel, I love you so much and am thankful everyday that you have helped make this all possible. Love you Iman, Bailey and Tony. To Tam and Hush Boutique, thanks for keeping my arm fly. To the best editor in the world, Leslie Allen! I love you to death and appreciate your honest feedback and encouragement. You are amazing!

Thanks to the entire LCB author roster, especially Tonya Ridley. I love your honest opinion about my books and always appreciate your help. To Kellie, once again, thank you for the hot cover. You are so talented. A big thanks also goes out to Tasha and the many test readers who worked on this project. Each one of you are truly appreciated.

Now, to my loyal readers, thanks for your patience during this process to create another fan fave. I'm thankful to each of you and know that without you, my success wouldn't be possible. If you loved The Dirty Divorce Series then hold on to your seats and get ready to take a journey with new drama, new characters, and new life lessons.

Be on the lookout for the Paparazzi EP on ITunes featuring Miss KP, XQuiz, and Kristine West November 2012.

Much Luv and Hugz,
Miss KP
www.miss-kp.com
www.facebook.com/misskpdc

Kennedi-1

"Ahh, ooh yeah. Damn, you 'bout to make me cum. You want me to cum don't you?"

"Un-huh," I lied as Harry forced himself down my throat.

"Keep doing it just like that, girl. Damn, you good. Do it just like I taught you. Go 'head. Oooooooh. Suck that shit."

"Stop, Harry! Stop! Pleaseeee," I begged through tear filled eyes.

He thrust his body deeper inside my mouth causing me to damn near throw up. I figured if I didn't spring into action he'd punish my mouth all night. He'd choke me too, or pull out his thick belts and prized spiked whips. My skin cringed at the thought. Since he wasn't a fan of having sex with me while I was on my cycle, sucking his dick until he came in my mouth was normally the plan.

Finally, my thin arms reached for him wildly with the intent of doing him harm when my alarm sounded. *What the fuck,* I mumbled as I jumped up in a cold sweat, scared shitless from another nightmare. Obviously there was no escaping the trauma I'd experienced as a child. The pain Harry put me through all those years haunted me daily.

The tears flowed as usual as I climbed out of my king-sized bed thinking about Harry and Tina Johnson. My foster parents were the worst people I'd ever come across, and the main reason why I hated my twin sister, Kasey, so much. They adopted us when we were eleven years old and basically ruined my life. Ecstatic and truly happy to finally be saved were the way Kasey and I both felt the day we walked into the Johnson's beautiful home. We felt rich; like we'd made it to the big leagues.

Due to Harry's lucrative family-owned construction company and Tina's hair salon, money was never an object. Life had been so hard for so long and it felt good to finally be adopted by a family who wasn't in it for the check. Tina wasn't able to have children, but always fantasized of having twin girls, so life was great in the beginning. Finally, we had our own room and toys and no more sharing secondhand clothes and holey underwear.

As I walked toward the other side of the bed and looked down on my overnight guest I was hit with another horrible memory; the one that I dreamt about most. The theme song to *In Living Color* filled my soul loud and clear. Letting out a thunderous cry I thought back to the night Harry sodomized me and changed my life forever.

Harry grabbed the remote control and turned up the television so Kasey wouldn't hear me cry. He'd been using the television for three years to mask the sounds. Trying to take my mind somewhere, I remembered singing the *In Living Color* song in my head. It was the same time every Friday night when he watched all of the reruns from back in the day. He entered me rough and hard.

"Uhhhhhhhh. Stop tensing up, just let it go in, girl, damn!" he told me.

"Please stop, it hurts really baaadddd, ooooooooouch, ouch," I cried as he entered my anus, deeper and deeper.

"Stop squeezing your muscles. If you keep pushing it back out then I'ma have to put it back in."

All I could do was cry.

At the tender age of fourteen, I was being treated like a grown ass woman.

"Kasey's next if you don't quit your damn whining. Be a

woman, dammit. Take the dick!"

Harry's threats were common, especially all the talk about going after Kasey. He even threatened to put us back in the system if I didn't do as I was told. Trying to avoid going back to foster care, or have my sister molested, I complied. My sister was all I had. Since we were abandoned I had to do whatever it took to protect her. Of course he knew we both feared being separated. The older we got our chances for being split up were greater. The best thing for me to do was just comply.

"Oh shit, oh shit, ohhhhhhhh! I think I'm 'bout to cum!"

'Til this day I remembered the sound of his squeal like it was yesterday. He pounded my tender backside with more vigor while I buried my head as far into the pillow as I could. It felt as though my insides were being ripped apart. The pain was so excruciating I simply wanted to die. I thought about begging for mercy again when the door flew open.

"Hey Babe, I came home early because…"

Her face turned beet red.

Tina's anger could be seen across the room.

"What the hell is going on here?" Tina yelled.

Immediately, I became thankful that my prayers were finally answered. Tina had come to save me.

"Baby, I can explain. Um-um, ummmm," Harry stuttered. Fear immersed his face. "Baby, I'm sorry. She just kept throwing herself at me. I told you she was fast."

"He's lying, Tina!" I wailed. So many tears flowed, seeing was not an option. "He made me do it! He made me," I cried with humiliation.

Tina stared at us both in disbelief with her hands straddling her hips. For moments she remained silent as her face continued to lose color. Then I got the shock of my life.

"Go ahead, keep fucking. Don't stop on the account of me."

"Miss Tina, noooooooooo. Please make him stop!" I cried out.

"No, go right ahead. You want to fuck my husband like you're a grown ass woman. Go ahead while I watch you take that shit. Babe, you want me to hold her legs up?" Tina whispered in Harry's ear as if all of a sudden she was turned on.

"For real?" Harry questioned.

"Go ahead before I change my mind. Every husband deserves one threesome. Today's your lucky day."

As Tina took off her cardigan, she kissed Harry on the back of his neck and started to massage his shoulders. "Go ahead and get back in there," she whispered calmly then removed her red lace bra, the main reason why 'til this day I'd never wear red lace.

After she exposed her breasts, Harry entered me as Tina held my legs back as he pounded me harder and harder. All I could do was cry. I couldn't believe that Tina was actually turned on. She started fondling my breasts as Harry pounded me harder as if he was turned on even more. Tina removed her pants and then her underwear. Making her way up to my face she started kissing me. As she put her tongue in my mouth, bile rose up in my gut. I just knew I'd throw up.

"Ahh, yeah, Kennedi. Ahh yeah," Harry panted.

"It's my turn now, Harry."

As Tina straddled her legs over my face, she sandwiched her vagina over my face and started gyrating. I couldn't believe her. Her scent was worse than Harry's.

"What you waiting on, lick it," Tina demanded. I turned my face speedily from side to side trying to escape her scent. There was no way in hell I'd lick another female.

"Oh shit babe, I'm about to cum," Harry shouted! "Uhh-hhhhhh…"

"You came in her, Harry!"

"I'm sorry, baby. I couldn't help it."

Little did Tina know, it wasn't the first time. All of a sudden I blacked out and could no longer take being humiliated. Something came over me and I just started swinging with the strength of a bull.

"Get the fuck off me!"

"What's going on?" a voice sounded.

Kasey walked in puzzled. She was in a state of shock to see us naked. I'd never told Kasey what Harry was doing to me. She thought I'd lost my virginity to my boyfriend Timmy. The truth was, Harry was the first and only person I'd ever been with.

"Kasey, he's been raping me every Friday for the past couple of years and she's okay with it!" I blasted while running toward her at top speed for help.

Kasey frowned. "What the hell is your problem, Kennedi? Get off of me, you nasty slut. We're going to get sent back all because of your whoring ass!"

"Are you serious, Kasey?" I screamed with hurt deep inside. "I took this shit for you. How could you talk to me this way? I'm your sister."

"For me? This is just nasty. Oh God, we're going to get sent back. Why did you do it, Kennedi?" She said waving her hands in the air.

"For you Kasey. I love you. I had to protect you. He said you were next. I did it for you."

Kasey kept shaking her head. "You liar! Why do you have to be such a roller? We're going back to foster care for sure."

"You damn right you whores are going back! All I tried to do was raise you to be respectful girls and look how you repay me. You sleep with my husband, trying to steal my good dick!" Tina yelled, flipping the script. She then grabbed Harry's work belt from his pants.

Instantly, she began to wail on me. All hell broke loose and we were rumbling like chicks in the street. Kasey just stood there paralyzed with shock and fear. She didn't even try to help me. As I pulled Tina's hair and tried to take a chunk out of her face with my nails, she screamed for Harry to help her. Harry tried to get in between us as I swung wildly. The fact that Kasey didn't help me at all hurt me to the core.

"Stop, she's pregnant! You're gonna hurt the baby! Just leave her alone!" Kasey finally shouted.

My heart stopped. I couldn't believe that my own sister turned on me. She knew we were gonna figure out a way to get rid of the baby; together, just she and I. She swore on her life she wouldn't tell a soul.

"She's lying," I remembered saying while shivering like crazy.

"I'm not lying. You told me not to tell," Kasey replied.

"Pregnant? You pregnant, girl?" Harry asked. His eyebrows were doing tricks.

"Is this your baby, Harry?" Tina's nose spread and a nasty scowl stretched across her face.

"You couldn't get me pregnant all these years, but you fucking get her pregnant! I'll fix your ass, Kennedi. You want to fuck my life up after I rescued y'all from that hell hole. Now, I see why your damn crazy Chinese Mama ain't want you. Got damn mutt, I'm gonna stomp that baby out of you."

In a fetal position I rocked back and forth as tears streamed down my face. Humiliation was an understatement. All of a sudden everything went from bad to worse. Tina's foot lodged straight into my face. Blood started to flood from both my nose and mouth. There was no doubt my nose was broken. The taste of blood filled my mouth as I laid face down on the tan carpeted floor. Blood leaked everywhere. Another blow came from behind forcefully into my back.

"Stop, stop, stop it!" I hollered, balling up trying to protect myself as much as possible.

"Get up whore and make me stop!" Tina lashed out. "You wanna be grown? I'll show your ass grown. If I can't have his baby what makes you think you will?"

There wasn't an ounce of fight left in me. My body shivered and I no longer had any control. All of a sudden another thrust channeled its way toward me, this time straight to my stomach. Suddenly my body went into shock and blood gushed from between my legs.

"Tina, you gonna kill that girl! Let her be," Harry tried to defend. By him opening his mouth it did nothing but make matters worse. Tina didn't give a damn. She was out for blood. As I laid there in shock, she continued to stomp my helpless body with no remorse.

"Kasey, help me. We're all we got. Help me, please, Kasey, please," I stuttered. My eyelids got heavier and my body throbbed with excruciating pain. Defeat covered every inch of my body while Kasey remained glued to a corner. She just stared at me.

"You're supposed to be my sister," I remembered mumbling.

Those were my last memories of that night which now haunted me on a regular. That was the day that any bond I had with Kasey died. No longer did I have a need to protect her or anyone else. The fact that my mother had given us both up to the state and that my sister betrayed me left me emotionless. I now cared for no one or anything.

Malcolm-2

Last night was crazy, but all I could think about was the amount of doe I blew. From gambling to tricking off on some groupies, reality set in and now it was time to go home to my family. Party over. One of my business partners wanted to meet with me in Vegas about opening a nightclub out there. My one-day business venture, turned into a weekend of bottle popping and hoe hopping. Meeting him this past weekend was perfect since Floyd Mayweather was fighting. Groupies were ready to give it up. Champagne and a little music was a great way to meet over business and set up another way for me to make even more money than I already had. Making money was just my style.

This popular groupie chick hung out with me all week-end. Everybody that was anybody in the industry had run through her. Was she really worth the fight that was coming with my wife about missing my flight yesterday? Hell yeah. That girl had the best head on the entire West Coast. Listening to my wife, Charlotte, fuss and argue for a few days was worth that good shit. Charlotte would get over it as soon as she laid eyes on the new gold spiked Christian Louboutins I brought her back from Vegas.

Pulling out of the parking garage leaving LAX, my phone was going off like shit. My wife had been calling me nonstop since my plane landed this morning. To keep a clear mind, I figured it was best to ignore her calls and deal with her once I got home. After looking in my rearview mirror it was time to uncover my eyes from behind my Chrome Heart shades. A night of partying showed in my blood shot eyes. There'd been no time set aside for sleep. It looked as if I had a week's full of a luggage under my eyes. My bed was calling me.

Driving into my gated community, finally reaching my house, I typed in my code to open the gate. It was best to park in the circular driveway so I could high tail it straight to the bedroom. If I entered through the garage, no doubt, Charlotte would be sitting in the kitchen as usual waiting for battle. The fact that my Bentley windshield had just been replaced last month was a lesson learned. Her anger cost me a couple of stacks and I wasn't in the mood this morning for another cordless phone being thrown through my shit.

Quietly putting my key in the door, I immediately heard her footsteps approaching as her heels click-clacked in the foyer.

"Who the hell is this whore, Malcolm?"

Here we go again, I thought.

Charlotte held up a picture of me with the girl I was with this weekend that she'd obviously printed off of the Internet.

"Bring your ass in the office right now. Let's see how you deny this one. I already have the laptop set up for your cheating ass."

The damn paparazzi had got me again. I was caught but there was no way she was getting me to admit a thing. The blogs and media had a field day with my ass on a regular basis. Ever since I started dabbling in the world of hip-hop, Malcolm Fitzgerald was the talk of the town. My name rung bells, but sometimes I wondered if the money was worth it. My once wholesome wife definitely changed and had become very bitter. Charlotte's insecurities had gotten worse and worse over the years. She went ballistic on a regular basis now. Sometimes I wondered who was worse, Charlotte or Tasha from the movie *Why Did I Get Married?* They both knew how to research and find shit.

The headline read:

Jet-setting Again Without Wifey, Hip Hop Business Mogul Malcolm Fitzgerald spends the weekend with the biggest jump-off in the industry. Click here, we have photographic evidence.

The first picture was of us partying at Tao, but the last picture was of me in bed asleep in my boxers. The tattoo of my daughter's face on my arm was a dead giveaway. That slut bitch had set me up.

"Come on, Charlotte, it's obvious somebody set me up," I pleaded, hating that she was in my office, my sanctuary.

"I'm tired of this shit, Malcolm. You're not going to keep embarrassing me. What type of husband are you?" Pain filled her face. "Do you realize you have a daughter? Suppose I was in the media every other week messing around on you. How would you feel?"

I simply shrugged.

"You knew what you signed up for when you tried to get with me twelve years ago. If it's so bad for you, then do what you gotta do. I get tired of your continuous complaints." I tried my best to keep a straight face as I flipped it all on her.

"Last time I checked you were the one pressed to get with me," Charlotte shot back. "Don't forget the real deal and who made all this shit possible," she said, waving her hands in the air.

"If you really believe that, stop complaining all the damn time. It's not a good look."

"Complaining? Are you serious?" She stepped closer, getting all up in my face. So close her breath swarmed me. "You cheat on me and now you're the fucking victim. Kiss my ass, Malcolm!"

"You're mental!" I screamed stepping back.

"And you're full of shit. If you were a real man you would just be honest and admit your faults. That's what real men do."

I chuckled. "Really? A real woman with class wouldn't be on the Internet searching gossip sights to see if her husband was cheating. Do you know how many women would love to be in your shoes? They all want to be married to Malcolm Fitzgerald. You have it all Miss Charlotte. Let's trade places so you can be in and out of town making moves? I have to do this to keep you in the best. Just the way you like it."

"Fuck you! My father made all this shit possible. I would be okay with or without you."

"So, why are you still here?" I asked calmly, keeping my distance from her.

"It's simple. I want my daughter to grow up with both parents...and..."

"And stop throwing your father all up in my face," I blurted out. "I'm tired of hearing that drama. Show that you have some class."

"No sir, let me tell you about a woman with class. A woman who moves out of New Jersey where life was just fine with her upper class family to chase her husband's dreams. The same woman with class borrows money from her rich father constantly, to help hold her man down who makes dumb ass business decisions on a regular. This woman has plenty of class, but you just don't know what you have. Do you know how many athletes and actors approach me on a daily basis?"

"Well, go fuck one of them, Charlotte. Would that make you feel better?"

She got quiet before hitting me with what she thought would hurt me. "You don't ever want me to give you a taste of your own medicine. Let's see how you would feel to be humiliated in the tabloids."

"Fuck the media! You gonna let them dictate our happiness?" Charlotte had succeeded in getting under my skin. I'd go crazy if the shoe were on the other foot.

"Malcolm, I'm human. In what book does it state that it's okay for a husband to commit adultery? I deserve better!"

she yelled. Immediately afterward, a flood of tears ambushed her face.

Looking at my beautiful wife cry her eyes out was hard to bare. The goal was to make it all seem like her fault. Just because I couldn't keep my dick in my pants, a part of me felt bad. The sad thing was, being a one-woman type of dude was never my thing. Never.

Growing up, I was always protective of my mom and sister. I wanted nothing more than to be a good husband, but my father cursed me. Watching him cheat on my mother with different crack whores didn't help. His infidelity even drew my mom to her addiction for drugs. Somehow I turned into a womanizer by default and Charlotte was my main victim.

"Do you regret marrying me?" Charlotte asked in a calmer tone.

"Don't ask me that, you know I love you."

"I deserve better," she cried.

I truly loved Charlotte but my reasons for wifing her up initially, were a part of my get rich plan. When we started dating in college her innocence let me know I could trust her. There was no doubt my man Frankie and I got it in while we were in school, but I knew Charlotte's potential, so I kept her close.

When her grandfather died and left her a multi-million dollar inheritance from his construction company in Jersey, my vision to be the top Hip Hop industry business mogul seemed like a piece of cake. I'd always had numerous hustles going on, from nightclub ventures, to producing music videos and short films, dabbling in music here and there. Making partnerships with anyone good at getting money was my thing. If it didn't make money, it didn't make sense. But with money came the lifestyle; females throwing themselves at me.

Charlotte was right, she deserved better than me, but she was worth more than me on paper so there was no whore on Earth I'd let fuck that up for me. No matter how much shit I talked, she wasn't getting rid of me. It was damage control time. Now, it was time to flip the script and make her feel bad.

"You're right, Charlotte, you deserve better." I walked right up on her and placed an arm around her shoulder. "Do you want me to leave?" I asked, throwing my head in my left hand, faking as if I was upset.

She paused before responding. "No, I don't want you to leave." Charlotte turned to face me, gazing into my eyes. "Just honor our vows."

"I promise I'll do better, baby."

"Are you even attracted to me? You don't even look at me the same. Since we moved to L.A., you've changed. Since we got to your hometown, you've gotten brand new. You always go after those hoochie looking light skinned girls with big, oversized asses. Am I too dark for you? Am I too thin for you? Do you want me to get ass implants?"

I fucking hate when she talks like this, I thought to myself. Her lack of confidence was a turn off, but I knew that it was my fault she was that way.

"No baby, I love your beautiful mahogany skin."

"Then why do you always cheat with those red girls? What do I have to do to make you love me and only me," she sobbed.

My wife always had a complex about being dark skinned and hated when people told her she was cute to be dark. It didn't help that it was obvious by my choice in the women I cheated on her with that my preference was honey colored women. My downfall was exotic looking women. Charlotte was beautiful with high cheek-bones, almond shaped eyes, and thick lips. There was no reason she should have felt insecure. It was just she wasn't my usual type.

"I love everything about you. Your walk, your talk, everything."

"I know what it is, you don't like my haircut."

"Your haircut is fine," I lied.

She knew I hated it from the face I gave her when she came home with it. Out of anger she cut all of her natural long hair into a Halle Berry pixi cut. It was such a turn off when she acted weak. That was Charlotte's biggest downfall. Taking a deep breath, I reached over to hug her tightly.

"Come here, babe."

"Malcolm, why can't you just act right? What do I have to do, bleach my skin?"

"Come on, babe. Are you serious? Don't talk like that. I love you."

Caressing her body, I kissed my poor wife and escorted her to the couch as she sobbed uncontrollably. Placing my cell phone and keys on the table next to the couch, I got up and rushed to my luggage in the foyer to get the Louboutins. They were sure to make her smile.

"Here babe, I brought you something back." I rushed back in smiling.

When she saw that honey colored Louboutin box, her frown instantly turned upside down.

"So, does this mean you're guilty as charged," she said with a smirk, continuing to dry her tears with the back of her hand.

"No, I'm not. Now, open your gift." I never cracked a smile. Innocent until proven guilty.

As she opened the box her face seemed confused.

"What is this, some type of joke?"

"What are you talking about?"

"There's nothing inside Malcolm, just hotel soap and lotion in here. Wait, what is this? There's a note. *Thanks M, how did you know I was a size 39, XOXO!*"

"What?" I asked with confusion spread across my face.

"You fucking bastard! Just when I was about to believe your dumb ass!"

Within seconds, Charlotte started throwing all types of shit at me including my Apple Pro Laptop I'd just bought.

16 PAPARAZZI *by* MISS KP

Fuck! That groupie had stolen my wife's shoes. *Damn!*

Malcolm-3

Welcome to Atlantic City, I whispered to myself as I exited my business partner, Frankie Sabatino family's private jet. It was the one-year anniversary of our club Black Diamonds so I was summoned by Frankie to attend the celebration. That was the least I could do since I hadn't been to Jersey in a while and owned twenty percent of the club. I was looking forward to seeing how the business was going.

Frankie Sabatino, my Sicilian homie had been a good friend since college. At first I hadn't planned on going to the Black Diamonds' one-year celebration, since scheduling had been so hectic. But when Frankie called me yesterday and told me his family wanted to have a huge dinner tonight, I got on the jet without one question asked. You don't miss a Sabatino dinner, especially if you were personally invited by Frankie's Uncle, Sonny. He wasn't wrapped too tight, so I always tried staying on his good side.

Frankie's family owned most of the lucrative businesses in Jersey and owned the other eighty percent of Black Diamonds. Our club ventures helped launder their money and my connections in the entertainment business kept the feds off their backs. The relationship worked great; especially since the Sabatinos were deep in the Mafia. That didn't bother me since my involvement was just to keep their club money looking clean. With my name attached, the Feds had no clue they were my business partners. This was my start for taking over the East Coast. There was no way I could turn Frankie down on this business venture. Making money was my middle name. It was a definite win for everyone involved; I was just waiting for my return on the investment.

How does this woman manage to annoy me all the way from the west coast, I wondered as the doors to the jet opened? The moment I turned my phone on, the badgering and annoying texting began all the way from the west coast. There were over twenty messages from Charlotte, but the last one took the cake.

If you and Frankie decide to fuck groupies this weekend, use a condom.

There was no way I was going to respond to that shit. She was still tripping off of what happened on my last business trip. On a better note, I checked my voicemail and I had a message from the love of my life, Gianni.

"Hi Daddy. I can't wait to go to the zoo tomorrow. I love you."

Guilt filled my heart. I had to cancel our plans for the zoo so I could come to A.C. I was definitely gonna make it up to my baby once I got back in town. Just before I was about to make a call, Frankie called.

"Mallie-commm, Mr. Lover- Lover."

"What's up, Frankie? I just landed."

"Okay, well my driver should be waiting for you in the terminal. How was the ride on the family jet? They treat you good?" he boasted.

"Most definitely."

"Cool. So, you ready to party after this business meeting?"

"Hell yeah, I know you got the ladies on ice," I said, ready for action.

"For sure. I miss my homie. You know I always show you a good time when you come here. We gonna do it big like we used to in school."

"The wifey letting you out tonight?" I joked.

"She don't have a choice," Frankie said quickly. "It's our

club's one-year anniversary. Times like this make me happy she's eight months pregnant. You know she would be trying to party with us to cock block."

"Well, you know I left Charlotte's crazy ass in L.A. for a reason. Wait 'til I tell you about her last episode."

"Some things never change. I'm sure she still can't stand my ass. It's your fault, though. You would always say you were with me when you were off on your missions." He laughed.

"If she can't get past things that happened over a decade ago, she's got issues. The hell with all that, we gonna do it real big tonight, baby!" I yelled.

"No doubt. I'm ready but mannnnnnnnnnnnn, I gotta tell you, Uncle Sonny isn't too pleased on the return and the clientele. He wants to discuss it tonight at dinner."

My body broke into an instant sweat. Frankie knew not to tell me until the last minute that his Uncle Sonny wasn't happy about the decline in business. I was terrified of that man. The last time I was in town, I witnessed him cut one of his employee's balls off for taking a smoke break while he was supposed to be working. He just wasn't the kind of man you crossed. My heart fell in my stomach with the thought of having to meet with him. Usually Frankie handled any dealings with Sonny.

"Is he upset with us?" My voice stammered a bit.

"You know him, he's always upset about something. I can count on one hand the amount of times I've seen him smile, and that's when he was ordering a death. That young wife of his keeps him miserable. He knew damn well he had no business marrying a woman in her thirties. He's more than twice her age. All that silicone makes a good showpiece. That bitch ain't shit though. She's a whore."

"So, does she step out on his crazy ass?"

"Hell yeah. He just can't ever catch her. She's slick as shit, but he loves her. The bitch is bad, though."

"Well, I'm trying to get the meeting over with, not look

at his wife, and party so I can get back home."

"Don't worry about my uncle. He'll be cool."

"Alright, see you in a bit."

The small Atlantic City airport was packed more than usual. There were a lot of rich kids traveling on their family aircrafts. As I maneuvered through the crowded terminal, I spotted my driver. He was a short well-dressed Italian man holding a card with my name.

"Hello, sir."

"Malcolm Fitzgerald?" he asked with a puzzling expression. Maybe he wasn't expecting a black guy. A good-looking black guy at that.

"Yes, that's me."

"The boss requires that I check identification," he said firmly.

"Oh, no problem."

Reaching into my Louis Vuitton wallet I pulled out my ID. That type of scrutiny was expected anytime I dealt with Frankie or anyone else he ran with. That was Sabatino protocol.

"Okay, we're good to go sir," he said with a nod.

"Cool."

The ride to The Borgata Hotel was very quiet. As I made a Henney and Coke, the nervousness I felt was hard to mask. With the news of Sonny wanting to meet with us, of course changed my thoughts about my visit to Atlantic City. I was trying to show face, maybe hit a couple of chicks, and get back to L.A. Now, there was no way my time in A.C. would be pleasant.

The first time I met Sonny, he and Frankie's dad, Frankie Sr., got into a huge fight over a card game. When alcohol's involved deep feelings were usually revealed. Old beefs came up and none of the nine others around at the time tried to mediate the situation. There were ruthless threats thrown back and forth so much that I thought I could've been killed for even looking at either of them. Unfortunately, for Frankie, before the end of my trip, Frankie Sr. was in a fatal car accident. My boy was devastated and really hadn't been himself since his father's passing. I just prayed that Frankie had been handling the business while I'd been in L.A. There was no room for error.

Gathering my thoughts, I prepared myself for the worst as we pulled up to the hotel. After checking in I made it up to my room to grab a quick hour nap before dinner. As I opened the door to my suite for a minute my initial thought was that the clerk had given me the key to the wrong room. There were two busty Italian brunettes having their way with each other.

"Oh shit. Sorry, I have the wrong room."

"Malcolm, right," one of the girls laughed as she walked over to me and started rubbing my shoulders and chest.

"You're a lucky guy. I'm Cherry and she's Mandy. Frankie told us to prepare you for dinner. Appetizers on us." They both laughed as they got back to business and continued kissing each other.

Frankie was known for these types of stunts, but I didn't mind…at all. *There goes my nap*, I thought to myself.

"He's cuter than I imagined. Do you play basketball? How tall are you?" Cherry said, as she played with Mandy's pussy eyeing me.

"I'm six foot three, and no, I don't play ball." I laughed while unbuttoning my white linen shirt exposing my six-pack. Cherry wanted me to fuck her and I was going to do just that.

"I want to suck your cock," Cherry demanded.

"So do I," Mandy moaned as if she was going to be left out.

"I'm not one to do much talking ladies. What y'all trying to do," I said, exposing my dick. I was eight inches soft. Their eyes bulged as they admired how big I was down there. Seconds later, both Cherry and Mandy made their way over to me and began to suck me off.

"I need that big black cock inside of me," Cherry begged.

"Hold up, let me get a condom," I quickly suggested.

"I got you covered," Cherry said sexily.

Usually there was no way I would use any chick's condoms, but we were in the heat of the moment and I wanted to tear her white pussy up. She was nasty and I wanted to fuck the shit out of her. Cherry was a beautiful girl. She kind of reminded me of that chick Megan Fox from the movie, *Transformers* and I wasted no time fucking her fine ass. I did just that and enjoyed every moment.

After over an hour of fun with the girls, it was time to get ready. We exchanged numbers and I invited Cherry to join me and Frankie later. She was the nastier of the two and I didn't mind seeing her again.

As soon as the door shut, I switched into business mode. There was no way I was going to be late for this dinner. I pulled my Gucci black, custom-tailored suit from my garment bag and laid it across the bed. I was meticulous about my gear and had to be sharp at all times. After a quick shower, I attempted to get dressed in a hurry until Frankie called to let me know he was already downstairs. It took me about ten more minutes before I could get down to the front of the hotel. Of course he had the flashiest car outside. His fire engine red 458 Spider Ferrari was souped up with rims and any other extras you could imagine.

I smiled from ear to ear. "Always clean! What's up my dude?"

Frankie got out of the car and greeted me with a big hug looking just like Rob Kardashian. He was dressed in all black as well, however his jewelry had much flash. He was iced out. From his ears to his neck, even his watch would blind you. Business must've really been good, but I just hadn't seen the profit yet.

"Hope you enjoyed your appetizer," he said, laughing wildly.

"Man, Cherry was the business. She got a nice ass for a white chick, too. I invited her out to the club."

"Guess I'll take Mandy then," Frankie joked. "Now it's time to paint the town. Let's bounce!"

The ride to Sonny's house was quicker than usual, due to Frankie's relentless speeding. We had less than fifteen minutes to catch up, me learning all about Frankie's latest infidelities. I never got my chance to come clean after realizing we'd pulled into an upscale neighborhood with eye-catching, monstrous-sized homes. As we pulled up to the gated mansion, Frankie punched in a code while I watched the gate open slowly. Nervousness infiltrated my body once again.

"I thought this was a big dinner? There aren't many cars out here," I said uneasily as the Ferrari sped up the driveway.

"Weird, right? It's 8:55. Uncle Sonny said to be here at nine and not to be late, so I'm not sure what's going on."

We parked, hopped out and strutted inside after being greeted by an older frail doorman.

"Hello, Fred. How's it hanging?" Frankie joked.

"Oh, Frankie. It's still there," he laughed as they gave each other a kiss on each cheek.

After I was introduced, we made our way through the humongous foyer to the dining area. It was very dark and gloomy but full of rich knick- knacks. The décor reminded me of a rich castle in Beverly Hills. The windows were floor to ceiling with heavy burgundy drapes and gold rope tie-backs. The furniture looked as if it belonged in an ancient museum. There were statues of lions, but what stood out the most was the huge portrait of Pamela, Sonny's wife. She was beyond beautiful; had my nuts on fire.

Once we approached the dining room, sounds of loud roaring, laughter and loud talking could be heard. It was definitely a celebration going on. Once inside, my eyes zoomed in on the long, twelve foot table of food. There was pasta, fruit, vegetables of all sorts, quiche trays, caviar and any meat you could imagine. Food was plentiful but strangely after we walked in, the laughter stopped. There were six older white gentlemen sitting around the table and one heavy-set younger black dude.

Who the hell was he, I wondered? He stood out like a sore thumb. Maybe he was an enforcer or something.

"Frankie, Malcolm, let's not waste any time. Have a seat," Sonny announced in his raspy, intimidating voice.

"What's up, Uncle Sonny?" Frankie replied.

"Hello, Sonny," I added.

"Yeah, yeah," he waved his hand and then started to whistle. "Marty, Marty, come now kitty."

His giant black and white tiger ran in the room and sat beside him submissively. You would have thought he was a dog the way he listened to his command. I couldn't believe this crazy dude had named a tiger after the zebra on Madagascar.

"What the fuck?" I whispered under my breath as I sunk in my seat.

My heart fell to the pit of my stomach wondering what he would say about the club progress. Sonny was never a fan of underachievement, so I just didn't understand him laying out a spread for our one-year anniversary. I took a deep breath hoping I was thinking too much into the situation and just decided to scan the room again. Unfortunately for me, as soon as my eyes set on Sonny, his were on me, too.

"So, Malcolm how's the hoppety world?" Sonny asked as he petted Marty on his head.

"Uncle Sonny, it's called hip-hop," Frankie corrected.

"Frankie! You don't correct me!" Sonny slurred. You could tell he'd been drinking.

Frankie bowed down respectfully as Marty circled around a few times before sitting again. Amazingly, Marty got up as soon as Sonny's voice loudened.

"Umm, the hoppety world is quite lucrative," I said,

fearfully after watching Sonny pick up and admire an oversized butcher knife.

"Well, please explain why I'm missing over two million dollars if the hoppety world is so lucrative. Why hasn't this Black Diamonds spectacle of a club made me any money? Where is my money, Malcolm?" he asked, slightly raising his voice and gliding his forefinger up and down the chrome blade.

"Sonny, I haven't been here since we opened," I stuttered. "I mean I invested a half of a mill that I haven't seen either. This type of investment takes time, right Frankie?" I asked, waiting for him to try and save me from the wolves.

"Uncle Sonny, I've worked around the clock to make this business successful. I've brought Malcolm in for many reasons, but the main one is obvious. His hands are clean. That's what we wanted, right?" Frankie chimed in.

"Stop your bitching, Frankie!" Sonny blasted. "Spending money and losing money doesn't work well for me. Malcolm, this is on you now. Make me my money back."

"Uncle Sonny, Malcolm and I are partners. Don't put it all on him. I brought him in on this," Frankie added.

Sonny waved his left hand. "Stop your whining!"

Before Frankie could respond, the overweight mysterious looking black dude whispered something to the old, bald guy next to Sonny. He then glared me down from head to toe. The scar over his left eye looked as if someone tried to slice his head open. Sonny acknowledged the guy with a nod and continued.

"Frankie, my nephew, what is the one rule the Sabatino's live by?"

"Loyalty and honor," Frankie answered.

"That's right. So sit back and relax. We are going to watch a quick video and then let's talk. Fred, tell my darling Pamela to join us."

"Yes, sir," the doorman complied.

Moments later, Pamela sashayed in the room with confidence. She was even more beautiful in person and knew she was the shit. Her long blond hair was flawless. Everyone drooled as her Double D's spilled from her white, flowing dress. She couldn't be a minute over thirty. What was a young girl like her doing with Sonny? He had to be pushing seventy.

"Hello, my beautiful wife," he said to her with a wide grin.

"Hello, sweetheart," she replied as she greeted Sonny with a long passionate kiss before sitting in the last empty seat to my right. Frankie's look of disgust was obvious. He must've really hated her.

"Let'er roll," Sonny demanded.

As the projector screen rolled down from the ceiling everyone directed their attention to the front of the room. In no time the video started and I was in a state of shock at what came across the screen.

"Come on Pamela, suck this big cock. You like this young dick don't you? My uncle could never fuck you the way I do. Say it."

"Oh yes, Frankie, you're the best. Enough of this put it in my tender ass…"

My eyes bulged at the sight and the eerie feeling that stung the room. That explained all the anger. Frankie was having an affair with Sonny's wife. Why was I here, to witness this shit?

"Now Pamela dear, explain to me. Why is it that my money isn't too old for you, but my dick is?" Sonny asked his wife.

"Sweetheart, he made…"

"Shut your whore ass mouth. You slut dame! Frankie, what do you have to say for yourself?"

Of course Marty was up again strutting heavily across the floor, behind Sonny. For some reason he kept eyeing me.

"Uncle, I can explain…" Frankie tried to say.

Sonny nodded. "I'm listening."

"Sweetheart, this is all a mistake," Pamela said eagerly. "He offered me an E pill and I had no control. I was gonna tell you, I swear darling, I was," she pleaded.

"Bitch, stop lying," Frankie belted with both fear and anger.

"Why did you do it, Frankie? Why did you dishonor me? You are a disgrace to the Sabatino name," Sonny said.

"I'm sorry, Uncle. I'm so so sorry."

"You're worthless just like your father."

"What?" Frankie's look of fear instantly turned into anger and then he lost it. "Yes, I fucked her. It's the obvious. But your wife wanted me. What do you want me to say? It was wrong but at least we know she's not trustworthy. I'm not the only one in here she's fucked," he announced.

"You're the only dumb ass that got caught," Sonny fired. "So what do you think should happen now?"

Frankie started sweating profusely. As he attempted to get up, Marty stood up and started growling. Something told me to stay my ass in L.A. I'd never been so petrified in my life. I kept twitching in my seat, praying Sonny wouldn't think I knew anything about the two of them.

"Sit down, you disloyal scumbag. How dare you dishonor me? Where is your loyalty?" Sonny questioned. His voice got louder and louder with each word.

The other five gentlemen at the table sat in silence as Frankie and Sonny went back in forth. Pamela tried to defend herself, but the conversation got so personal her words were unheard. A lot of hurtful things were said and suddenly the obvious was revealed. It was personal.

"You want to know why I fucked Pamela?" Frankie stood and shouted, even though Marty's growl was overbearing. "It's because you fucking killed my father! You bastard!"

Sonny displayed an evil smirk. "And now I'm gonna kill you."

"I would never give you the satisfaction," Frankie said

before pulling out the .357 caliber magnum from his waist. It felt like I was watching a scene from Scarface.

"Kill him now!" Sonny demanded.

Every man at the table drew their guns, but before they could shoot, my best friend put the gun in his mouth and took his own life with one shot. The sound was horrendous and the blood sickening. Frankie's blood splattered across my cheek. His lifeless body fell to the floor as blood poured like running water from his mouth. His piercing green eyes stared at me as I sat paralyzed with fear. In complete shock, I couldn't believe what I had just witnessed. My college buddy laying in cold blood right before me and there was nothing I could do to help him. My life flashed before my eyes. All I wanted to do was get home to my daughter Gianni.

"My God, Sonny. What have you done?" Pamela cried.

Before she could speak another word, the black heavy gentleman looked over at Sonny as he smiled. I knew what was coming. He stood from the table as another gentleman handed his 9mm gun to Sonny. The black guy then grabbed Pamela with his burly arms as she tried to fight back. He was huge and there was no way she could escape his grasp.

"Pull up this whore's gown. Open her legs," Sonny demanded without hesitation. "You wanna fuck a big young cock, do you? Can't get no better than this, bitch?"

The smallest guy in the room sprung into action, opening Pamela's legs as I sat glued to my chair scared shitless. As Pamela's shaven vagina was exposed Sonny stood for the first time and walked over without remorse. Before I knew it, he took his 9mm and shoved it straight up Pamela's pussy. She screamed and screamed so loud I became nauseated at the thought of the pain.

"Come on, Pam, fuck it!" Sonny taunted. "You want it in your ass now?"

"Stop it, Sonny. You're sick!" Pamela pleaded between squirms and ear piercing sobs.

"Shut up, whore!" Sonny yelled back.

Everyone in the room watched the drama as if it was business as usual. I was the only one uncomfortable with what I was witnessing. Sonny lifted her body and shoved the wet gun into Pamela's ass. She let out a huge scream louder than the others.

"Sonny, no! I'm sorry, please don't. I love you. Please don't do this to me!"

There was nothing Pamela could do to save herself. She begged Sonny for forgiveness, but there was no turning back. After fucking Pamela in her ass, he let off two shots. Shit and blood flew everywhere silencing her instantly.

"Your pussy wasn't that great any way," he said after wiping his nose with the back of his hand.

There was an instant stench that filled the air. Marty started going crazy, jumping around excited as if he was in the wild where he belonged. The sound of my heartbeat reigned through my pounding chest. The visual of two dead bodies was more than I could handle. Suddenly, vomit erupted from my core. Sonny then walked over to me and placed his shit filled gun to my temple. My heart raced as I wondered, why *was I next?*

"Get yourself together, Malcolm. I'll let you live, on one condition."

"Yes, Sonny…" I could barely get my words out. "What's that? What's the condition?"

"I need my money, plus interest. You have twenty-four months to turn this shit around. If you love these beautiful women in your life you won't breathe a word to anyone or what you witnessed," he said as the Christmas card that I sent to Frankie the year before, illuminated on the projector screen.

My eyes had tripled in diameter. "Most definitely, sir. Most definitely."

"Fellas, feed these maggots to Marty in the back. There's no need to waste all this disloyal meat."

This must've been routine because Marty couldn't contain himself as he started to snap at Pamela and Frankie's bodies. All I could think about was if I was really gonna make it out of Sonny's house alive.

Kennedi-4

My sex was the bomb and I knew it. It was something about my pussy that kept niggas sprung. *That girl is bad*, I whispered to myself looking in the mirror admiring my beautiful hazel eyes and flawless skin. My beauty mole under my lip made many weak at the knees. After washing the sin off my body from a busy night, I got out of the shower and slipped on my robe over my negligee. Pushing up my D cups to give even more cleavage; I blew a kiss to myself and sprayed my Love Spell fragrance all over me. Now that I was refreshed, I had to keep my word and check on the breakfast that I'd promised to make.

Making my way down to the kitchen it was obvious something was burning. The water in the pan was damn near gone. I was irritated as hell because I was geeking for round two. *How the hell did I burn the boiled eggs?* Suddenly, startled by the sound of keys coming through the door, I dropped the pot on the floor.

"Shit!" I yelled as the water burned my leg.

Just when I thought I was about to be put back to sleep with pleasure, my morning shot straight to hell. My heart pounded against my rib cage at the sight of my family. My first thought was to run up the stairs, yet I just froze.

"Mommy! Mommy!"

"What the fuck are y'all doing home so early?" I asked my fat ass boyfriend, Sharrod and my five year old son, Chase, as they waltzed through the marble foyer. Shocked and nervous as hell I didn't know what to do.

"Why you all dolled up at seven o'clock in the morning?" Sharrod questioned.

"Huh? What do you mean? Can't a girl just look sexy without being questioned?" I fired back. Somehow I knocked over a mug spilling coffee all over the granite countertop.

"And when the hell did you start drinking coffee?"

I remained still. There wasn't much I could say. There was no good answer and I prayed Sharrod didn't realize how nervous I was. He'd flip, whip my ass, and possibly kill me if he knew what I was up to.

"So, what's the point in coming back early?" I asked as loud as possible. I hoped like hell my voice echoed to the upstairs bedroom.

"Mommy, I have to tell you all about our trip. We had fun," Chase interrupted all excited like I really gave a fuck.

"Chase, go sit down," I instructed harshly.

"Nah lil man, go get ready for school. That's why I got you back early."

As usual, Sharrod's stern voice overrode everything I said. The moment I watched my son's feet rush toward the staircase, I panicked. I couldn't allow him to go upstairs.

"Chase!" I called out.

"Why you so damn jumpy, Kennedi?" Sharrod stepped my way.

"What are you talking about? I'm not jumpy."

"Yes, you are. You jumpin' at every noise you hear like you nervous or some shit. What you been doin' since I been gone? You been givin' my stuff away? Come here, let me feel it."

Before I could even move, Sharrod swiped his hand against my vagina like someone swiping their credit card through a machine.

"Whatever, you tripping," I lied, swatting his hands off of me.

"Well, show me you been good and I'll give you what daddy brought you back from his trip," he teased with a little black box.

Any other time I didn't mind giving up a little ass for a nice gift, but today was not the time to try and get a new trinket. Quickly changing the subject to avoid giving him some, I flipped the script. There was no way his tiny penis was gonna fit in me after the week I had with that anaconda upstairs.

"Babe, I'm tired."

"Well, I'm not." Sharrod's tone was stern. His words were spoken with authority as usual. "Come on and take care of your man. Chase, go up stairs and get yourself ready for school."

"Why he gotta go upstairs? Chase just go down in the basement and play your Xbox or something until we're done," I urged.

"Yeah! Thank you, Mommy!"

Before I could even blink, Chase was out of sight and Sharrod started fondling me, disgusting me to the core. My heart raced, unsure how I'd get him to leave the house so my boo could escape, without getting two slugs to the chest. Sharrod was fat as hell, but merciless in the streets. He was a known killer and had war marks to prove it.

"Give me a kiss," he told me.

Trying to play it cool I kissed him; anything to keep him from suspecting anything.

"That's my girl," Sharrod said, smiling showing that damn chipped tooth that irritated me. "You smell so good. Damn! Damn, Damn!" he kept saying.

My mind drew a blank. Jittery as hell, I jumped as soon as Sharrod touched me between my legs again. I couldn't fuck him. He would know someone else had been inside me. I kept trying to think of an excuse not to fuck. But once he picked me up onto the counter his little penis was instantly at attention. Since he was being so persistent, kissing me up and down my neck, I gave in. My actress skills went straight into effect the moment he got inside me.

"Ahh, ahh, yeah daddy!" I faked as Sharrod pounded his fat into me. If it wasn't for his money, his wanna be Big Poppa ass would've never been able to snag me a couple of years ago, so fucking him never excited me.

"Turn over," Sharrod demanded like he was really breaking my back.

If I had a choice, I would rather crawl through nails for money then to have him pounce on top of me. Besides, my wet warm pocket between my legs was getting dry by the second.

"Turn over for what, nigga? Your big ass better hurry and cum or you gonna be short!"

"Bitch, you must be trippin' all the money I spent on yo' ass at Short Hills Mall before I left. You betta turn around and earn your keep."

Rolling my eyes, I turned over and of course that little pee-wee kept slipping out. This dude really thought he was doing something as he continued to talk shit.

Sometimes I wondered to myself, *is this nigga really serious? How could he even think that he was really hurting something with that Vienna sausage of his?* Imagining he was Carmelo Anthony, I started to throw the ass at him at a rapid pace. I knew he liked nasty talk so I did what I had to do.

"That's right daddy, cum for this pussy, I love this dick daddy!" Anything I could think of I said to try to get that fat motherfucker to cum.

"Uhhh...Uhhh..." he grunted. Just as he was close to squirting, my crumb snatcher burst upstairs from the basement.

"Mommy, I'ma be late for school!"

"Damn, Chase!" Sharrod yelled, annoyed as hell.

He never raised his voice at his pride and joy so he must've really been upset about not getting that nut off. It took everything inside of me to hold my laugh in.

"Saved by the bell," I mumbled as I quickly slipped my

Betsey Johnson robe back on. This was the one and only time I looked forward to getting Chase ready for school.

"Mommy, everybody is already walking to the bus stop," Chase whined, looking out of the window as if that was gonna make me move any faster. Lord knows I didn't sign up for this shit anyway.

I rushed over to the laundry room and grabbed a pair of pants from the floor. "Here put these on."

"Kennedi, I told you to start gettin' his stuff together at night so you wouldn't have to scramble to find uniforms in the morning."

Ignoring his comment, I watched Sharrod pull his pants back up while I'd decided to purposely make Chase miss the bus. I knew Sharrod would have to take him at that point.

"Here, put this shirt on."

Before Chase could even reach his hand out, the shirt went flying through the air as Sharrod's face frowned.

"Bitch, what kinda mother are you? Why would you have him put on this dirty ass shirt with dried up ketchup all on the sleeves? You triflin' as shit!"

"Well, wash it Sharrod, since I'm so bad," I returned.

"Man, I bought twenty uniforms so that my son would never run into this problem. Here it is the first week of October and he don't have a clean uniform, which means you haven't washed one time."

"And your point is…"

"Yo, Kennedi if you say one more word out that smart ass trap of yours, I swear to God I'ma knock your fuckin' teeth out!" Sharrod threatened, getting all up in my face.

I knew I needed to chill cause the nigga was definitely trigger-happy. He'd been bragging relentlessly before he left for his little trip about some guy he smoked for making him look bad in front of his boys. I never agreed with none of the gangsta shit he pulled regularly, but since I was in it for the money, it didn't matter.

"Sharrod, you better get the fuck out of my face. I told you about doing that shit in front of my son."

"Damn, I snagged the wrong twin," he snapped, deliberately wanting to hurt me. "I bet Kasey would've appreciated being up in this big house and having my son."

That shit struck a nerve. "Go be with her then! Y'all probably fucked before anyway."

Brushing me off, Sharrod was determined to make his point, "Man, you cute bitches kill me. Just because you Chinese and black you think you the shit. You think you the baddest bitch I ever had. Man you better check my track record."

"I'm not half Chinese, I'm Filipino mixed. All Asians aren't Chinese ignorant ass." I got right up in his face.

"Mommy, no, stop!" Chase whimpered before making his way between us.

"Boy, get off me," I said, pushing him away.

"But, Mommy…"

"I said get back, Chase." I kept my evil eye on Sharrod as my son ran back to the window.

Sharrod backed up. He was a violent nigga, but I could be a violent bitch when needed. I was sure he didn't feel like being rushed to the hospital again. The last time we had an altercation, I stabbed him, leaving him with thirty-five stitches in the chest.

"Aweee, man, the bus is gone!" Chase shouted.

"Well, since your daddy loves you so much, let him take you to school. Come in here and eat this popcorn. Get something on your stomach."

"But, Mommy I want cereal."

"We don't have any milk. Besides, you don't need all that sugary Frosted Flake shit. You wanna be a fat ass like your daddy? "

"Bitch, stop talkin' to my son like that!" Sharrod belted.

"Why don't the both of y'all just get out?"

Just when I thought Sharrod was ready to go, he was at

the island in the kitchen, at work cutting up some coke. That nigga didn't play when it came to his money.

"Man here, bag this," he said, throwing a bundle of cash in a rubber band on the counter. "I'll be back. I'ma run Chase to school."

Before I could respond, the front door suddenly burst open. All I could hear was a lot of rumbling. I didn't even have time to react before I was joined in my kitchen by not only the New Jersey State Police, but the FBI.

"Hands up, I need to see your hands right now! Out where I can see them!" a Fed yelled.

Next thing I knew my son was screaming and Sharrod was in handcuffs, being escorted back into the kitchen.

"So, look what we have here," a female Fed said shaking her head. She looked at me quite pleased.

"Get the fuck off me, you dike bitch" I yelled as one of the female officers tried to detain me. Continuously tussling with that bitch caused my robe to fall off exposing my naked body. I was completely humiliated.

"Where you're about to go young lady, you'll get used to dikes real quick," she fired back.

"Mister big time Sharrod, we got you for sure this time," the female federal agent smiled and continued to taunt him. "Damn, how is it gonna feel to be away from those tata's?"

My nerves were shot. Sharrod kept giving me the eye which told me to be cool. He had no idea why I was nervous. Little did he know, it had nothing to do with the Feds. I was more worried about what they were gonna find upstairs. Not even five minutes went by before my secret was revealed.

"Well, look at what we have here. Today's a two for one special," an agent revealed walking downstairs.

There was no way I was getting out of this one. Q was handcuffed, trying to pull away from the officer. *How the hell did I get caught up like this,* I wondered.

Q, Sharrod's best friend had been my fuck buddy almost

the entire time Sharrod and I had been together. But I never thought I would've gotten caught up like this.

"So, you guys were having some type of threesome with the little one in the house?" the female officer agitated.

Meanwhile, hell's fury had erupted in Sharrod's eyes. I could tell he was hurt. Disappointed. Angry. He still didn't seem to understand. Maybe he didn't want to believe it.

"Yo, Q, for real tho. What the fuck is you doin' here?" His voice was enraged and facial expressions beyond rigid.

"Sharrod, I can explain," I pleaded.

"This is gonna be good," the female officer instigated with a malicious smirk.

I wanted to slap the hell out of her. Why joke at a time like this?

Sharrod had gone postal. As he kept trying to break away from the police to get at Q, I leaned as far away from him as possible. His reputation as a killer was clear to me. I knew all the secrets about the murders he'd committed in the past. Q knew too, yet he kept his cool like everything would be okay.

"Man, she been throwing the pussy at me, so I had to smash. I was gonna tell you," Q responded.

My mouth flew open. Shock filled me. "Nigga, stop lying! Don't fake. We've been fucking for years if you want to keep it 100!"

"Money over bitches, Q! Ain't that what we always said, nigga?" Sharrod roared.

He kept squirming to escape the police officer's grip. "You ain't shit, Kennedi! You gon' pay for your betrayal, bitch!"

"Kennedi, my dear, your cheating ways helped us get both of these fellas at the same time, so we couldn't be more thankful. You guys are about to go away for a long time," the female agent stated with pride.

"I'd say at least twenty to life," a male officer added with a smirk.

Just when I thought things couldn't get any worse, Shar-rod looked at Q and then over at my son who sat on the floor crying uncontrollably. The words he blurted changed my life forever.

"Who going to jail for twenty to life? Those ain't my drugs. That's her shit! This house is in her name, not mine!"

Kennedi-5

Two years later...

"Oh my goodness, Shawn, damn that shit feel good."

"You know I'm gonna send you off right."

"Please don't stop, I love it, oh my goodness. I'm about to cum," I said, letting it all go.

"I know you gonna miss me."

"Put those big titties in my mouth right now."

I grabbed one of her breasts and sucked it as if it were a big piece of juicy watermelon. Playing with her pussy with my middle finger it was obvious that I hit her hot spot. She moaned and begged for me to taste her. Returning the favor was never an issue. Spreading her legs open as far as my little twin bunk would allow, I devoured my mouth between her lips and went to town. Never in a million years would I have thought a woman's legs would be wrapped around my neck, but I got the hang of it quick. Gotta give it to myself, I was quite the pleaser. After taking her straight to ecstasy her body fell limp and then she let out a howl.

"Woohoo! Shit girl. I'm a bad bitch if I taught you all that. What a great student you've become. Your head is the bomb," Shawn praised.

"I know. I'm gonna miss licking that pussy," I said, putting my panties back on.

"Excuse me ladies, what's going on in here," Mrs. Bates interrupted, almost catching us for the umpteenth time.

"Nothing nosey ass, I'm ready to get up out of here," I

snapped back, still holding a grudge against her for constantly giving me a hard time my entire bid.

You would've thought I fucked her husband or something. She hated me for no reason, but the feelings were mutual for sure.

"Watch your tongue young lady before you have a much longer stay."

"Whatever," I mumbled under my breath.

There was no way I was allowing that bitch to get under my skin. She was always after me, but loved Shawn to death. Sometimes I wondered if Mrs. Bates was on Shawn's payroll. They always looked like they were conspiring on something. Shawn insisted Mrs. Bates was her canteen hook up.

"Be easy pretty girl," Shawn smiled as she gave me a wink once Mrs. Bates walked off.

I rolled my eyes. "That lady makes me sick. If I didn't want to catch a charge I swear to God…"

"Kennedi, it's not that serious. Let it go. If you see her on the street one day, pull her wig off or something, but for now just chill."

I stared into Shawn's eyes knowing I would miss her humor.

"What am I gonna do without my road dog on the streets? You always keep me calm."

"I'm right behind you. Just the way you like it," she laughed.

Shawn always knew how to relieve my stress and make me feel better. There was no way I would ever say that I was gay, but while I'd been locked up being with her got me through those lonely nights. During the day we were BFF's, but bumped pussies at night. She was the best sex I had since Q. That was what I would miss about her most. Nasty and adventurous, she brought out things in me that I didn't even know existed. Her exotic look and Jamaican accent made me want her constantly. Shawn was a cute girl and I would've never thought she was into women if I saw her on the streets. We had a strong attraction for each other that was hard to explain. I loved dick, don't get me wrong, but a girl had her needs.

Shawn was in for some felony fraud shit and was one of the biggest dealers in L.A. Of course I landed the woman with the most status in the prison. Who knows how I got so lucky. What was the likelihood of her being my cellie and taking care of me my entire bid. She had so many connections still on the outside world that I had no need for anyone on the streets. Shawn was my savior in that hell hole. We had a lot in common so it made it easy for us to get along.

I remember the first time we met when I got here. There was a huge chip on my shoulder and I didn't trust anybody. Sharrod had just betrayed me and I had just finally finished my case. I got moved across the country from New Jersey to a women's facility in Chowchilla, California. Being moved to the west coast definitely took me by surprise, but I felt maybe this was where I was destined to be for a new start.

When I first got here, I'm sure during our first encounter I rubbed her the wrong way, but it wasn't long after that she proved to me that she was a true ride or die chick. Shawn finally broke me down after I ignored her for almost a month as if she didn't exist. After a few nights of childhood flashbacks, one night in particular got Shawn's attention. At last someone was able to break through my tough exterior.

"Stop, leave me alone! Get off of me," I yelled before waking up in a cold sweat. As I glanced over at the next bunk Shawn was wide awoke.

"You ready to talk yet?"

"Huh? What do you mean?" I asked, rubbing my eyes.

"For the past couple of weeks I haven't gotten any rest because of somebody named Harry attacking you in your sleep. Who the fuck is Harry? I'm ready to beat his ass my damn self."

I couldn't do anything but laugh at not what she said, but

how she said it.

"No, I'm good."

"What the hell is so funny? I've barely got any sleep since you came in here?" Shawn complained.

"What's your problem? Why are you so nosey?"

"Sweetheart, let's make one thing clear. I'm a boss. Boss bitches ain't nosey they're aware. I could really care less."

"So, why all the questions?" I remembered balling my face up.

"What's your story? I need to know if I can trust your ass, or if you just another bitch that just breezes through," she continued to pry.

"For what? We can do our time without being friends."

"You young girls kill me thinking the world owe you something."

"What's that supposed to mean? I might be twenty-two," I spat, "but I've been through a lot for my age and seen enough to teach you some shit. I'm a boss myself, Miss."

"Well, act like a boss. Real bosses seize any opportunity to get where they need to be. I'm an opportunist and if we can ride together that's a plus. If we can't then that's cool, too. Just want to let you know this, whoever the fuck Harry is, he's a problem and he's fucking up my rest."

"Harry was my foster parent that raped me for years as a child. Satisfied?"

Before I could stop myself the words spilled out. It was the first time I'd ever said it aloud, but it felt good.

"I'm sorry. I didn't know, I just thought he was…"

"Yeah, just like I thought, you don't know what I've been through."

"Look, I'm not Harry. I'm not the devil who did those awful things to you. For some reason I'm drawn to you and I don't know why. I'm not the enemy Kennedi, you can trust me."

"Trust you? I don't trust anybody."

"Seen your kind before. You think the world owe you something?"

After a couple of hours of shit talking, Shawn was able to break me down. How, was a mystery to me. After all of the years of the pain and frustration, I was finally able to let go of my tears and allow somebody in. Shawn just held me and allowed me to bear my soul.

For once, someone was genuine and made me feel they had my back. What she said to me about her loyalty rang true. I never really trusted anyone, but for some reason Shawn was easy to talk to. All my life I'd never really opened up to anyone fearing the perception of being weak. That night I opened up to a complete stranger. My life had always been a mystery to everyone. My sister Kasey and I hadn't spoken again about what happened at Tina and Harry's house. The nightmares continued since there was so much bundled up inside of me, but after letting go and opening up to Shawn my life changed. Sleepless nights were almost extinct. Instantly, I felt a connection with her.

Not only did I open up about Harry, I even told her about my mother and how she refused to take my sister and I home to her Asian family. Shawn was shocked at all I'd been through growing up. Once I told her about how she left us at a train station rest stop when we were seven, Shawn cried with me. The fact that we were in and out of foster care until we were fourteen years old and letting her in on my darkest secret that I was molested, helped her better understand the wall I put up.

Shawn felt sorry for me just like my Big Mama. I went on to tell her about how my father's mother, Big Mama was our savior. She found us a couple of years before I met Sharrod. She tried to repair as much damage as possible and raise us the best she could, but I always had my own agenda. Never before had I really spoken in detail about how my father was killed when we were ten years old and we'd never met him. Not even to Sharrod. He only knew of stories my Big Mama would tell him when he would go over her house complaining about me.

Just when I started to feel vulnerable and guilty for talking too much, Shawn opened up to me as well. She let me in on how she was a millionaire due to fraud and ran a huge drug cartel in L.A. She was well respected in Cali. An emotional night turned into an ongoing relationship for two years that would soon to come to an end.

"Why are you looking at me like that?" Shawn asked, finally breaking me out of my trance.

"You're special. I just don't know how you were able to break me down and get me to trust you. I don't trust nobody out here. You're different. Everyone in my life that I ever let in always betrayed me. They let me down every time, but you're different. You always had my back."

"Say no more. I'm gonna miss you, too." She smiled and gave me a huge hug.

"Shit, we've done everything together for the past two years. It's just gonna be weird." I put my head down trying to control my emotions.

"Now, you ain't getting soft on me are you?" Shawn asked.

"Never. I'm just happy to get out of this place," I said, regaining my composure.

There was no way I was gonna break down. Now, it was time to close this chapter. Life on the outside was my focus. With a second chance, nothing was gonna stop me from being on top.

New Jersey was my past. There was nothing in my life that I wanted any parts of and I was ready for a new start. Shawn knew that I had no intentions on returning to Jersey, so she made connections in L.A. to get me set up and on my feet with a dude named Ray. They were really close and he respected her. When she spoke to him it was as if she was giving him an order, but then she would get soft and warm. It was no telling what was up with them, but I didn't care. With Shawn only having a few months left on her bid I was excited to have my road dog soon join me. Since I really didn't roll with too many girls on the street, the first time having a true friend that I could trust felt good. More than ever I was ready to start my new life leaving everything and everyone behind.

It was 8:30 a.m., and I had to be at Receiving and Discharge by nine. Shawn and I only had another a half hour together before I had to leave.

"Okay so remember, once you get out of here you're going to be picked up from the bus station. Now, you know it's well over four hours in a car, so it might take you damn near six and a half hours with all the stops. Ray is on board and knows to have your ride there at 5:30 p.m. to pick you up. They have all your new identification cards that you need," Shawn advised.

"Oh my goodness, this shit is for real."

"Damn right. Now, stay focused. It's important if you ready to leave this old life behind you, remember your new name, Ashley Jacobs."

"Ashley Jacobs. Okay, I like it."

Shawn smiled. "You ready for this."

"Yes, I am. I feel so grateful to you and owe you the world Shawn, really."

"It's all good. I know if I ever need you, you'll be there, Ashley."

"What?"

"Girl, you better get used to your new identity. Don't fuck up all my hard work, Ashley Jacobs."

She smiled again and gave me a tight hug. "Repeat after me, Ashley Jacobs."

"I got it. No worries, Ashley Jacobs."

"Also, I had a hook up in R&D so your take home package is set. You got some money in there. You should be cool for at least a week. Once you get to L.A., Ray got you until I get home in July. It's not that far away."

"Muah, I'm gonna miss you," I said, blowing a kiss. Shawn snuck a glimpse of my phat ass as I prepared to leave.

"Ashley, what we did in here is between me and you. Remember nobody can know about us."

"We're on the same page with that. I love you, Shawn."

I shocked myself because I'd never told another person that I loved them and meant it. Not even my son. Someone finally succeeded with breaking down my wall. We hugged one last time and had a long passionate kiss before I was off to receiving and delivery for my release.

Once I got there the process went smooth. After I checked in with C.O. Bates, she handed me my package so I could go get dressed. Breaking it open, I was eager to see what Shawn had sent for me to wear. Even though she was well off, it was sad how Shawn lacked style. Of course the fashionista in me was a bit concerned. Fall in L.A. was different from what I was used to. But surprisingly, she kept it really simple with a black fitted t-shirt, a black baseball cap, black leggings, and a black pair of low top Adidas. There was also a thin, black fitted Kenna T leather jacket. I was cool with that. Reaching further in the box was also a Gucci fanny pack that had over $1000 and a cell phone.

All I could think to myself was, *how did Shawn pull off getting me a cell phone?* As I strapped my fannie pack around my waist, it felt like I was ready to go on a caper with all my black. As C.O. Bates escorted me down the long walk to the gate, I reflected back on the past two years of my life.

"So, where you headed?" C.O. Bates asked.

"L.A., the land of the famous."

"Well, you be safe out there young lady and don't let me see you back in here."

"C.O. Bates, I know you don't like me, which is cool, so stop acting like you care. For the record, we won't cross paths again."

Now I didn't give a fuck since I was going home. That

lady had given me the blues for the past two years.

"You never know. You might need me one day."

I shook my head. "I seriously doubt it old lady."

"Oh, we'll cross paths again Kennedi Kramer, I'd put my life on it."

"Nothing wrong with having confidence C.O," I replied before throwing up the peace sign.

The fresh air hitting my skin was refreshing. As I watched the black iron gates slowly open, I took a deep breath and inhaled as much of the morning dew as my lungs would allow. The sound of birds chirping and the smell of clean cut grass were all things I took for granted all these years. Stepping over the freedom threshold felt good and I was ready to really live life. Listening to the gate screech as it started to close with me on the other side was a good feeling. Before getting on the van to go to the bus station, I closed my eyes and took it all in.

Never in a million years would I have thought that getting inside of a van would be so exciting. For the first time in a longtime nervousness came over me. I was so close to my new life in L.A. and was so afraid something would go wrong. Anxiety was getting the best of me. Just to put on a seat belt felt good to me. All the little things that I took for granted seemed to matter to me so much. Starting a new life was scary, but I knew I didn't want any parts of anything associated with Sharrod. Too bad for Chase, I didn't want kids anyway. My new life had officially started as Miss Ashley Jacobs and I never wanted to look back.

Kennedi-6

Looking at the time on my cell phone I couldn't believe it had already been over five hours. As I looked around the bus and saw the different types of people, I wondered what their stories were. It made me realize even more than ever, you never know what people have been through in their lives. Looking at the old man across the aisle from me who had slob dribbling down his mouth, I wondered what his story was. With his cigarette behind his ear and arm permanently bent, it was an instant reminder of my Big Mama. Due to her addiction to smoking she had multiple strokes. She was the main reason why there was no way I would ever smoke. The bus was filled with many different walks of life and smelled like piss and funk. I was so ready to be in L.A.

Staring out of the window, I thought about the morning when my life changed for the worse…when my war with Sharrod began. I could admit that I was wrong for messing with Q. It probably killed Q to listen to me fuck Sharrod that morning. It was the fourth time he had to hide upstairs with fear of getting caught and I felt bad every time. Our affair had been going on for the majority of the time Sharrod and I were together. No matter how he faked to Sharrod once we were exposed, it was all a front. He loved me just as much as Sharrod.

My intentions were never to be with Q for that long, but we were so passionate together that we just couldn't help ourselves. Who would've thought that the FBI would be the ones to expose our affair? But now all that shit was in the past.

Fuck both of them niggas. Now, it was all about me.

Breaking from my daze, reality set in again that I was finally free. It had been a long two years, thanks to Sharrod. Last time I heard, he was locked up in Fairton, NJ. Who would've ever thought that his fake ass would flip on me? If he thought I was going out like that, he was truly mistaken. Facing twenty to life was never a part of my life plan, and because of the Oscar worthy performance I put on the court stand, the judge only gave me twenty-four months. His ass got twelve years, so in the end I was the one who made out.

This was one hell of a bus ride, I thought.

Being in the same seat for hours was no fun, but as I looked out of the window I was flabbergasted at how Los Angeles was even more beautiful than I'd anticipated. Moments later, the bus driver finally came over the loud speaker with news I'd been waiting hours to hear.

"Good Afternoon passengers, our next stop will be Los Angeles East 7th Street station. Please gather your belongings. We'll be approaching the terminal in approximately ten minutes. Thanks for choosing Greyhound and have a nice day."

Thank God. I couldn't believe it. I was almost out of my hell and approaching heaven on Earth in less than ten minutes. As I gathered my things a noise in my bag caught my attention. It was my phone.

It had been so long since I heard a cell phone ring I almost didn't realize what it was. *This has to be Shawn checking in on me*, I thought to myself.

Fumbling through my bag, I desperately tried to find the phone before I missed the call. After finding it and glancing at the unknown number on the screen, I knew it was Shawn for sure.

"Hey baby, miss me already, huh." I answered excitedly.

"Oh, we'll be together soon bitch, trust me."

"Who the hell is this?" My mood instantly went south.

"Who the fuck you think? The nigga that's going to

spend the rest of his life huntin' your ass down like a fuckin' K-9 until I catch you! But trust me, it'll be sooner than you think."

"What?"

I couldn't believe it. It was Sharrod. I hadn't heard his voice in two years.

"How the hell did you get this number?"

"Don't worry about that."

"Fuck that, Sharrod, I need to know."

"Nah, what you need to be worried about is how I'ma murk your ass!"

All types of thoughts ran through my mind. If the phone was in the package Shawn had given me, I couldn't understand how Sharrod could've got the number. It just didn't make sense.

"You better start sayin' your prayers, bitch," he added.

He was starting to piss me off. "If you still mad about me and Q, you need to get it over it. I guess you see now that he wasn't really a true friend. If you wasn't so far up my sister's ass, then maybe Q wouldn't have gotten this punani. You just got what you deserve, Boo-Boo."

"Fuck you and Q! Guess you didn't make his funeral, huh? Nigga got killed in the pen. Guess he underestimated me."

My eyes widened. "Q's dead?"

Sharrod laughed. "Yeah, that nigga dead…six feet under where you're gonna be. You must've forgot who the fuck you snitched on!"

"No, I know who I snitched on. A bitch-ass nigga!"

"You think that shit was cool letting the Feds get in your head and convincing you to go state evidence on me. I got connections everywhere."

"Be the big boy that you are and do your time, you fat bastard!"

"You hot bitch. Hot bitches don't last on the streets, you fuckin' whore."

"Just because I fucked Q doesn't make me a whore. Maybe disloyal, but never a whore. Come on Sharrod be real,

you can't blame me for fuckin' him. Your sex was some shit."
Everyone on the bus seemed to be looking at me by now, but I
didn't care. "Again, how the hell did you get this number?"

"You're so fuckin' stupid. If I can have you watched in
prison, I can touch your ass on the streets for sure. Trust me."

"And what does that suppose to mean?"

"Does C.O. Bates ring a bell? Well, she's my aunt."

My blood started boiling like lava. That old fat huzzy
had a nerve to be Sharrod's aunt. No wonder she stayed mind-
ing my business all the damn time. That shit made me want to
personally get in the driver's seat, turn the bus around, and
whoop her ass all up and down the prison's hallways. Sharrod
went on and on and then finally he struck another nerve.

"She told me you were dyking up in there."

"Looks are deceiving babe, but anything other than your
lil' pencil," I shot back.

"Bitch! I'm comin' for your ass! Bet that!"

"Whatever, nigga."

"And when was the last time you seen your son?"

"I haven't seen him since I got locked up and don't plan
on seeing him anytime soon. He doesn't need me, he'll be fine.
Hell, I survived without a mother. His lil ass would slow me
down anyway."

"I got somethin' for your triflin' ass, little do you know.
You get out of prison with no intentions on gettin' my son from
your grandmother. That was the only thing savin' your life."

"You should've never got me pregnant. You know I
don't do kids. That was my way of getting further in your pockets. Okay now, I'm exposed. I used your ass! There, I said it.
Now, you take care of the little boy you wanted. Damn, my
bad, you can't because you at least gotta do ten more years last
time I checked. By the way, how's that ass? I know some Bruno
looking dude probably blowing your back out. Now, get the
fuck off my phone."

"Bitch, your days are numbered. You don't really know

me like you think you do. I got connections."

"Are you threatening me while the Feds are listening? That's smart, let me be the reason you lose your phone privileges."

Click.

Before I could finish cursing him out the phone hung up. I know his fat ass was mad as hell. *How in the world did he get my damn number*, I wondered again?

Now, I was starting to question if I should've refused the witness protection program. Yeah, Sharrod was pissed at me, but I had to do what I had to in order to hit the pavement. With all his connections on the street there's no telling how he was able to call my phone. Was it C.O. Bates, who knew? Obviously, I had to watch my back.

No doubt I was wrong for fucking his best friend, but he didn't have to try to give me the wrap. If he didn't try to put that shit on me when they ran up in the house, then maybe he wouldn't be in the situation he was in now.

The FBI showed me pictures with Sharrod on dates with different chicks. He even took one girl on vacation to Maui. He'd never even taken me further than Miami. All that time I thought I was living the good life as Sharrod paraded different chicks out of the country.

Shawn taught me what living the good life really was with her different stories about traveling the world. She'd been so many places; from Paris to Dubai, and even South Africa. That was the life I was determined to get. I knew I had what it took to live life to the fullest. All I had to do now was just find my next meal ticket to fame and fortune. L.A. was the place to get it and I had nothing to lose.

Excitement flushed through my veins and I couldn't get off the stinky bus fast enough. As it finally came to a stop, and I made my way off, I pulled out the phone number for the guy I was supposed to call. The phone rang once, then went straight to voicemail.

What the fuck, I thought.

I started to question if this was all some fake shit that Shawn had sold me while I was locked up? Was she really who she said she was? My blood started boiling the angrier I became until my phone rang from an unknown number. Something told me it was Sharrod calling back for round two.

"You fat fuck, I don't have time for your bullshit!" I answered.

"Who ya talkin' to?"

I paused for a second at the man on the other end with the thick Jamaican accent. "Who the hell is this?"

"Is this Ashley?"

"Oh yeah, is this Ray?"

"No, he sent me for you. I'm on da corner of East 7th Street in a black tinted Range Rover."

"So, where's Ray?" I asked suspiciously.

"You wanta ride or not," the caller shot back.

"Look, I don't even know you."

"And me don't know ya either."

I had a bad habit of never trusting anyone, but I figured I'd better chill.

"My bad, I'm just new to town and not sure who to trust. I see you. I have on a black baseball cap. I'm coming across the street now."

As I ran across the street to the truck, I noticed a tinted black conversion van start to drive at full speed. Irritated as hell with the rude non-driving fool, I sashayed across the street to let the bastard catch a look before I threw up my middle finger. Right as I approached the passenger side of the SUV, several shots were fired.

"Oh shit!" I screamed before jumping inside the truck.

This dude who'd come to pick me up was obviously ready for war because by the time I jumped into the passenger seat, he was firing back with his Glock and pulling away at a high rate of speed at the same time.

"Ya got a bill on ya head aye, gurl!"

"I don't know anybody out here!" I yelled while ducking down as much as I could. Glass shattered just before blood gushed everywhere. Oh my God, was I hit?

Kennedi-7

When I looked over at Ray's man he was bleeding profusely from his shoulder. Thank God it wasn't me.

"Oh my gosh you're bleeding!"

Ignoring my concern, he weaved in and out of traffic as
if he was never hit. You would've thought he wasn't in pain,
and an expression of fear was nowhere in sight. This shit
seemed like it was normal to him. Anger was definitely fueling
his engine, but being afraid was obviously not an option. My
emotions were all over the place. My dreams of living life with
the big leagues in L.A. wasn't going down the drain because of
this niggas beef. Just that quick my life could've been taken
away for nothing. There was silence for the remainder of the
ride.

Twenty minutes later we arrived at our destination, The
Playa's Mansion. This must've been the spot where I would
meet Ray. All I could think about was what type of shit did
Shawn have me caught up in.

As soon as we walked in the door Nicki Minaj's song,
Beez In The Trap blazed through the speakers. It didn't take me
long to figure out we were in a strip club when we walked in
and I saw a girl with a pink wig on stage shaking her ass like a
tambourine.

Ushering me to the bar, my driver was still bleeding.

"Sit here. Ray will be witcha in a bit, aye."

"Are you gonna be alright?"

He ignored me as usual and continued walking to the back of the club. I was amazed at how he'd just taken a bullet and acted as if it was business as usual.

As soon as I sat at the bar, the bartender came over to wait on me.

"You must be Ashley."

"Excuse me. Have we met?"

"No, but we've been expecting you. What are you having, it's on Ray?"

"I just came home so to be honest, I have no idea."

"Okay, I'll whip you up one of my specials, and by the way I'm Isis."

She gave me a wink and then strutted away hard like she was trying to flirt. I might've done my thing when I was away, but I was truly on the prowl to get me a lottery ticket, a dude with a bag. There was nothing Isis could do for me but get me free drinks.

"Taste it," Isis said, licking her thick lips, as she brought me over a mixed drink that had a yellowish color.

"Umm, it's good, what's this?"

"A Coco Loco. Coconut Ciroc with a mixture of my own island fruit juices. Welcome home mama, have another one."

After downing four more drinks along with three shots of Patron, I was feeling nice. It seemed as if a weight was immediately lifted. I was a free woman, and it felt good.

"Ray's ready to see you now," Isis said.

"Okay, but I'm gonna need your help," I said, stumbling off of the bar stool and falling flat on my ass.

"Girl, you can barely walk. Ray is gonna be so irritated," Isis replied as she helped me off the floor.

"What the fuck was in that shit, Isis? Did you slip me a mickey or something?" I asked as she helped me to the office to meet the guy who was supposed to help me get on my feet.

She just ignored me as I stumbled, falling into her a couple of times as we walked down the long, dark hall. I wondered what type of island juices she'd put in that damn drink.

It felt like I walked a mile before we arrived at Ray's office. It was very dim, and reeked of weed and incense. There was also a lot of Bob Marley framed art on the wall. Isis helped me to the chair sitting opposite of the large oak desk.

"Baby Girl, ya drunk?" Ray asked in a heavy Jamaican accent before even spinning around to look at me.

He was the most handsome Jamaican guy I had ever laid eyes on. Dark brown skin, with pure white teeth, and a bald head. He looked like a handsome ass rough neck. There was an instant rush to my clit. He was man candy that I wouldn't mind getting with.

"What…she can't talk. Is she drunk, or did ya give her someting else," he said, looking in Isis' direction. Blinded by beauty I tried to get myself together.

Isis winked and let out a laugh. "I gave her some of my special juice."

"Ya put some magic dust in her shit. Gurl, ya crazy," Ray replied.

"I'm a little tipsy. You had me waiting for so long," I said, feeling like I was fading in and out.

"Me brother was shot, so I need to know who tryna kill ya."

"Look, Ray no disrespect. You don't know me and I don't know nobody in L.A., so y'all ain't about to give me that beef."

"The word is dat ya baby daddy tryna hit ya head. So, let me know before I help ya."

"My son's father is in prison. I just came home today, so I have no idea why we were shot at. I'm just trying to move on with my life and get paid. I've been down for two years and I'm just trying to get back on my feet."

"Ya tryna get paid. Take your clothes off. Let me see what ya look like under all dat black," Ray instructed.

"Excuse me?" I slurred.

"Ya gotta pay for dat shit. Me brother could've died. Ya have to earn ya keep 'round here. Let me see ya body. Come on now. Time is money. Ya need another drink to get comfortable."

For some reason I was feeling horny and didn't have a problem with showing this complete stranger my body. I didn't know if it was the drinks, whatever magic dust they were talking about, or if it was the fact that I was turned on by his bossy approach.

As *Party* by Beyonce pumped through the speakers, I felt the need to give a slow strip tease for Ray. His sexy ass turned me on. Even though he had a scar down the right side of his face that looked like someone tried to sever his cheek, he was still sexy as hell. Blood rushed to my clit and made me feel as if I wanted him inside of me. Gyrating to the music, I felt the urge to fuck.

By the end of the song all of my clothes were on the floor, and Isis was sucking on my breasts and fondling me between my legs. She really wasn't that cute, but was very exotic looking with a hell of a shape, so I guess that's what kept her employed.

"Stop, Isis. I don't want you, I want him," I said, drunkenly pointing at Ray.

Instead of joining us, he just sat there and bobbed his head to the music, watching Isis continue to fondle my body. Not knowing what had gotten into me, I started fingering myself and placed my fingers in Isis' mouth.

"Taste good, huh," I asked while rubbing my juices all over her lips.

Isis grinned. "Like fruits and berries. Ooh Ray, I like her. She's a keeper, and nasty, too."

"I'm not gonna fuck her yet. Ya can have her tonight Isis. After ya fuck her good, take her to da spot and get her set up. I don't want to fuck her when she's drugged up and drunk. I want dat pussy sober."

"Yes, boss," Isis complied, before Ray left the room.

As horny as I was, I knew I needed to be fucked and didn't care where the sex came from.

"Ashley, I guess it's just you and me in this big old office. I'm gonna make you love this tongue, now open your legs so I can taste that juice box."

No longer having control over my body, Isis had her way with me. Whatever poison Isis filled my body with took control. Finally, my thirst was quenched and I liked it.

Malcolm-8

Last night was another crazy night with my wife, which explained why I slept in one of the guest rooms. With pictures of me being posted on the blogs daily, as usual, she was tripping about another groupie situation. Normally, I didn't care what those dumb ass websites said about me, but this time I had to admit…I'd really fucked the wrong chick this time. She was almost as bad as Karrine Steffans. Why this hot chick wasn't playing fair blew my mind. A part of me wanted to call and curse her ass out, but I was scared it would just make things worse. This was the time I wished my sister was a fighter so she could whoop this chick's ass for selling the tabloids a story. There was no doubt I would see her again, it was just a matter of time.

Just as I made my way out of the bed to get my day started, my five year-old daughter walked in confused. She was the only thing in my life right now that made sense. Listening to her little feet patter throughout the house, I could hear her coming down the hall. When she walked in, all my problems disappeared.

"Daddy, Daddy! Why are you in here?"

"Hey princess, and why aren't you dressed for school?" I asked skipping the subject.

"I am. We're having a PJ party today."

"A PJ party."

Suddenly, the fun snatcher came in the room with much attitude ready to ruin our happy moment together. Any other time she would be downstairs giving our nanny Sophia her duties for the week. How does the old saying go, *misery loves company*.

"Come on, Gianni. It's time to eat so Miss Sophia can take you to school," Charlotte said.

"Mommy, I thought you were taking me."

"No, I have something to take care of with daddy before he goes away for a while."

Gianni looked at me with a confused expression. "Daddy, where are you going?"

"Princess, your Daddy isn't going anywhere," I replied. I hated when Charlotte told my daughter dumb shit like that.

"Are you still taking me to the park when I come home from school, Daddy?" Gianni questioned.

"Um, no sweetheart he's not. Daddy is not gonna be home for a little while," my wife interjected.

"But Daddy, you promised!" Gianni whined.

"Yes, I'm still taking you to the park, baby girl. Mommy just got the days mixed up."

"Yeah!" she yelled waving her hands in the air as she ran down the hallway.

"Stop running before you fall again!" Charlotte yelled out before she looked away from me rolling her eyes as hard as she could.

Sometimes Charlotte would get annoyed with Gianni when she was angry with me. She was jealous of how much I loved her, but the main reason was because she was my twin. My daughter looked exactly like me, from my brown skin, my wavy hair, and she even had my dimples. Her eyebrows were thick like mine and her toes were even shaped the same. She was the one girl that had my heart. Guess the saying was proven right. When you drive a woman crazy while she's pregnant the baby comes out looking just like you.

When my daughter was at home and awake was the only time there was peace. Charlotte wouldn't start a fight in front of

67 PAPARAZZI by MISS KP

Gianni. Her reason was she never wanted her to experience violence, which was some bullshit. She was violent towards me on a regular. The real reason was she wanted to keep fronting to her family that our lives were perfect. Since my daughter was at her parents' house so much she knew Gianni would tell it all. The picket fence tale was all Charlotte ever wanted. Too bad my lifestyle prevented me from being that guy.

After Gianni went downstairs it was time for her to start with her badgering again.

"Get out the bed and pack your shit."

"Whatever," I replied. "You say that shit once a week." It was time to ask my wife the question that could determine the course of my day. "Charlotte, all jokes aside, we really need to talk?"

"Jokes my ass. I'm serious."

"Did you ever get a chance to talk to your dad?" I asked, ignoring her last comment.

"Malcolm, I'm so tired of borrowing money from my father to fund your dreams. Why don't you ask one of your many hoes?"

"Look, I know you're mad at me, but this time I really need the money. It can be detrimental to our family. Time is of the essence. The business over in Atlantic City is still in jeopardy. I'm in knee deep with the wrong folks. We have to get out of debt or it can…"

"We? Negro, did you just say we? It's always me. I'm always bailing you out of some shit while you go around town sleeping with every floozy in sight. Just two years ago I bailed you out of those so called Atlantic City issues. Unless your ass was lying."

She was right. The last time my life was spared by the Sabatinos, she came to my rescue. But instead of paying the entire bill, I paid enough to buy time with hopes of things being better by now. There wasn't a day that went by that I didn't regret just using the money Charlotte gave me to get Sonny out of my life. History was repeating itself and the sleepless nights were back. Sonny was crazy and I wasn't trying to have him take my life like he did Frankie. Expanding in Jersey had been a big mistake. Now, Charlotte had to help me get out of this mess.

"Baby, if I ever needed this money before I need it now. My investors in Jersey are not happy and I need to make this deal come out of the red fast. They will kill me."

"Are you insinuating that your life could be at risk? Really Malcolm?"

"These guys are not to be fucked with. I watched them...Trust me I need the money." I hesitated. Charlotte never knew the details of what happened with Frankie.

"How much, Malcolm?"

"Ten," I mumbled.

"What the hell? Ten what?"

"Million. Look, I'll give your father his money back. I just need to get things back in order. You know I'm good for it. Just put your anger aside for the sake of Gianni."

"Don't you dare put Gianni in this!"

"Charlotte, I need you."

Finally, I felt a sense of relief when she picked up her cell phone. I had so much on my mind. Now, I understood why I married Charlotte in the first place. Despite all the other women I fucked, there was no other woman who'd been down for me the way my wife had been over the years, and I loved her for that.

Now, it was time for my Plan B money move. No matter how tired I was from a long night of arguing, time was money and no doubt the shower was calling my name. Today was a big day for me. I had to meet up with a buddy of mine, that I grew up with from Watts. He was getting major paper and was definitely a prospect for a new business venture. Since I had such great connections with some major networks it was a no brainer to create a pilot for a reality show, and collaborate with one of my man's top rap artist, Neko Luv. He'd already started creating a buzz in the industry and just needed that extra boost to get him on super star status. Business with him was simple. The days of watching sitcoms were dying by the second. With reality TV being the latest fad, it was the perfect business venture. I was all in.

After getting out of the shower, I went to my closet to decide what I should wear. This was definitely not the type of crowd I usually ran with, so I wanted to make sure that I wasn't too over the top with my attire. It was rare that I wore anything with a rubber-sole. Dressing fly was what I was known for, which explained the different endorsements under my belt from various fragrance companies to top of the line designers. The latest ad I'd done in GQ definitely put me in the forefront to land another run as one of the sexiest black men of the year in Essence Magazine.

It wasn't easy, but after contemplating over a couple of outfits, I decided to wear some jeans and a white Gucci v-neck sweater. The closest I was to a rubber sole was my Gucci boots. Once I was dressed, I took an extra look in the mirror and quickly noticed that my goatee needed to be cleaned up a bit. After throwing a towel over my shoulders and lathering up my face with shaving cream, I started to shave when all of sudden Charlotte came in like a bat out of hell.

"So, the slut still texting you, huh? I knew you were still sleeping with her."

"Man, what the hell are you talking about now?"

"The white bitch, Cherry. You told me you were finished with her over a year ago."

"Stop going through my phone, damn."

"Go to hell, Malcolm. See if I ask my father for anything else for your cheating ass," Charlotte said, throwing my phone, and breaking the mirror. Of course I cut myself with the razor trying to dodge the glass.

"You crazy bitch! You just want me to beat your ass."

"Make my day. You would be thrown in jail so damn

fast. Now, see how fine those sluts think you are with that big ass cut on your face."

"What real woman is jealous of her husband?" I asked.

"Jealous? Don't fucking insult me. Why would I be jealous of your gigolo ass? You need to learn how to keep your dick in your pants and then maybe we wouldn't have the problems that exist now."

"We have the problems that we have because you're so got damn insecure," I said, dabbing my face with alcohol. I went back to the closet to change my sweater since blood had gotten all over it.

"Did you ever stop to think that I have these feelings because of you? Like I said last night and a few minutes ago, you need to go."

"This is my house."

"Um no sir, this is my damn house! My father bought this for me, not you," Charlotte quickly corrected. "We need a break. That way your ass can fuck all the whores you'd like in your own space. You still have your condo downtown. Just stay there."

"Noooo…I'm staying here where I'm paying the bills."

"Guess I'm gonna have to call my father after all, to get you out of here because I want you gone."

"Call him, with your crazy ass," I shot back.

As Charlotte turned around and walked away with a little smirk, I knew she really was getting ready to call her father. *Shit, there goes my ten million*, I thought. Cherry had called at the wrong damn time. However, even if Cherry hadn't called, Charlotte was so miserable and evil nowadays, it was almost impossible to live with her anymore. Maybe she was right. Maybe it was time for me to roll out. On that note, I decided to pack an overnight bag so I could stay at my condo. Charlotte talked shit the entire time until I left.

As soon as I got in the car and pulled off, Cherry, my old side chick from A.C. that I hit from time to time was calling back.

"Hello."

"What's your deal?" she asked with an attitude.

"Babe, I really don't have any energy to fight with you today."

"It's obvious you aren't having a good day so all I have to say is that you need to keep your wife on a shorter leash. Her crazy ass really crossed the line this time."

"What the hell are you talking about? What has she done now?"

"I texted you last week letting you know that I was gonna be in L.A. When I got your response I should've known it wasn't you because it just said, *I don't care,* which didn't sound like you at all."

"I never got a text from you."

"Exactly. Your wife must've deleted it. I called you all last night to remind you that I was coming in town, and to see why you responded like that. Once I got to the airport I was told that my flight was cancelled. Now, I'm stuck in Portland because of your stupid ass wife. She called the airline, acting as if she were me, and cancelled my flight."

"Come on, Cherry, that's a little extreme. How you know it was my wife? You were in Portland. Maybe that's a beef you need to take up with your new Trailblazer boyfriend."

"Wrong. The bitch called me and bragged about the shit. She's crazy, Malcom, and I'm pissed off. I have a video shoot this morning and can't get on a flight for another hour. She's messing with my money now. I'm one model that's known for being on time and being reliable, so this shit is unacceptable. She's gonna pay."

"Cherry, don't forget who put you on and made you into the video vixen you are. I mean, what you want me to do? I told you I got a lot on my mind."

"Wire me some money for what I'm losing today. And an extra stack for my pain and suffering."

"Alright. I'll send you a couple of stacks to your account once I get to my meeting. Anything else you need, Miss?"

Cherry was just being difficult. She was paid out the ass now and was in high demand. There was no doubt she had no need for my money.

"Stop being stingy and give me some of that good cock when I get in town."

"You're tripping if you think I would ever hold back on you. Hit me when you land Miss Cherry."

"Don't get lost when I get in town and not answer your damn phone."

"You know where to find me."

"Cool."

My mind was on overload with all the drama in my life. On top of all the shit I'd been through this morning it was only 11:30 It felt like I'd already worked a full day, and I hoped shit would get better.

After fighting traffic, I made my way to the studio where we were hosting auditions for our reality show pilot. The amount of girls that surrounded the building was a good look. There were police everywhere to make sure everything stayed under control. I couldn't believe the response. Maybe it was gonna be a good day after all.

"Excuse me, you fine glass of water. What I gotta do to get a shot on this show. I'm down for whatever," this ugly ass groupie with a bright red wig yelled as I walked through the police barricade.

Ignoring her, I took a quick glance and realized quickly that the response that we got was not gonna get us any real money. It was important I didn't have my name attached to some ghetto bullshit.

As soon as I walked in through the back door, my man, Donovan was sitting there with a group of guys dressed in all red. It was obvious he was still into his same street shit. Usually, I was punctual when it came to business, but my morning was hell and I didn't want to start off business like this with my homie. My reputation when it came to making money was important to me, so I had to keep it real and let him know what happened.

"What's up, fam?" my man said.

"Hey, what's up? Sorry I'm late, man, wifey is tripping...*again*."

"What the fuck happened to yo' face pretty boy?" he said, laughing.

"Wifey happened," I replied, rubbing my scar.

"Man, the paparazzi havin' a field day wit yo' ass. How the fuck you deal wit dat shit? That bitch wudda been six feet fuckin' wit my homefront."

"That's what comes with this shit. Diddy said it best, Mo money, mo problems," I said, followed by a chuckle.

"I would have to kill one of them mafuckas for gettin' in my bi'ness. Come over here so you can meet my artist."

The closer I got to the crowd of dudes the stronger the weed scent became.

"What's up my man, Neko Luv, right?" I said, giving him a pound.

He just nodded his head while letting out a cloud a smoke. It was obvious they didn't even care about the police being everywhere as they continued to pass the blunt.

"You wanna hit?" Neko asked me.

"No, I'm good, let's get down to business. From the looks of the girls out there, we're gonna have to hit the strip club or something. Those chicks out there are rachet," I said, getting straight in business mode.

Immediately, I noticed there was a little lack of respect from Neko Luv, but I had to show him who was boss. They all were gonna know who was the head nigga in charge. I had to make it clear who was gonna help them eat. Without me, nobody made any paper. Once we got past all of the business side and they heard my vision on marketing him with the new reality show, it was all good. He was game and then it was on to the fun part. He made it clear that he didn't want to be looked at as a Ray J wanna be with the idea we had in mind, so we put a spin on the show. Instead of the girls just competing for love, there had to be a talent aspect as well. So, it would be a cross between looking for love and American Idol. We also decided to have the viewers play a part in who was chosen. They were sold on the idea. Now, all I had to do was figure out a way to get my wife to help fund it.

Kennedi-9

My mind was on overload wondering what the hell happened the night before. The so called Coco Loco drink had obviously participated in my lack of memory. Trying to ask Isis was pointless because all she kept saying was, "Girl, you're off the chain." Who knew what the fuck that meant? Who knew why my ass was sore? I didn't have any answers.

The only thing that made sense was I now had a roof over my head thanks to Ray. He was an asshole and a jerk indeed, but getting to his good side wasn't going to be a problem. I'd dealt with dudes like him before. I was blessed with the gift of gab, so it was never an issue for me to have a dude eating out of the palm of my hands. My survival mode had taught me how to keep a man. As long as you fucked 'em good and keep 'em fed, they couldn't help but fall in love.

The place was a hole in the wall and it felt like I was back living with my grandmother, but it would do for now. Looking around, I figured I could spruce up the place and make it my own after making a little money. But then again, for what? I didn't plan on being here that long. This shit was definitely temporary.

Needing to get a few things from the mall before it was time for me to hit the club, I jumped up and made my way toward the bathroom to get in the shower. The water was a rustic brown and I was so disgusted that I only took a quick bird bath and jumped back out. Since I didn't have many options for clothes I put on some black leggings, a Lakers tee, and a pair of

Uggs I found in the closet. I didn't know whose they were, but they were purple, a size seven, and they matched, so they were mine now. On my way out the door to catch a cab, my phone rang. The number was blocked, of course.

"Hello."

"Did you forget you have responsibilities here in Jersey?"

Once again I was completely shocked by the voice on the other end.

"Kasey?" I couldn't understand how everyone kept getting my damn number. The shit made no sense.

"Yeah, it's me," my twin sister replied.

"How the hell did you get this number? Who gave it to you?"

"Does it matter? What does matter is the fact that you're over on the West Coast trying to chase a fucking dream instead of…"

I instantly cut her off. It only took seconds for my sister to piss me off. "Look, trick, I know you want Sharrod. I heard about you going to see him in jail. You always wanted him, so now you can have him and his seed. I don't do kids and couldn't give a flying fuck about anyone in New Jersey. Don't call my phone again. You and everybody else are dead to me!"

Click.

There was no way I was about to sit and listen to her shit.

"Yes, can you take me to The Grove?"

Multitasking was my strong suit. Hailing a cab as I cursed out my twin sister was a piece of cake. Once again, my mind started doing flips on how Sharrod and Kasey got my phone number. Now, I started to question Shawn's motives. She and C.O. Bates were kind of close, so I wondered if she was working with them the entire time? Something was up and instead of trying to figure it out, it was time to get a new phone as soon as I got to the mall. Even though my pockets were on E and I was balling on a budget, the new phone was a necessity.

    With The Grove being one of the best outside malls I'd ever been to, my shopping trip was heart wrenching. Once upon a time I could go to the mall and pick up shit without looking at the price tag. Before today I'd never been in a Forever 21 or had to shop in the junior's department instead of the couture section. It was depressing and painful. After buying two new cheap shirts a pair of jeans and some underwear, a new phone had to wait. As bad as I needed one, I had to put it on the back burner until I made some cash.

    After window shopping at Barneys for hours, I finally caught a cab to the club with motivation to go back to get those Louboutins. They had spikes and lots of height which had my name written all over them.

    The cab ride to the club wasn't that long. When I got out and made my way inside the club, I wondered where Ray was. It was something about his Jamaican ass that turned me on, but I still knew he wasn't my ticket to get on. No matter how many strip joints he owned, I didn't come all the way to L.A. to let a strip club nigga wife me up. I needed some real money. He was a six-figure nigga and I wanted the big league. However, it was a must that I worked my mojo to use him until my come up came to light.

    My way of showing him what I was made of was me dancing tonight at his club. After making my way to the back, getting instructions from some of the veteran strippers on what costume I could wear, and putting on some makeup, it was almost time for me to take the stage. No matter how nervous I was, I knew tonight was the night that would determine my future. There was no doubt this Jersey girl had a lot to offer and had no problem with taking over the west coast. We knew how to make it pop, and I was determined to show Ray I was no

rookie, since that was what he conveniently called me.

As I waited for my turn, I thought it was best if I paid a visit to the bar to get me a drink to take the edge off, because deep down inside I really was nervous as hell.

"Looking good, Miss Ashley. You ready for your big debut?" Isis asked.

"Hell no, I'm scared shitless."

"I know your nasty ass ain't scared. You're an animal so you'll be just fine. As a matter of fact, take this and all your nervousness will disappear."

Isis handed me a blue pill. As nervous as I was, there was no time to contemplate on whether I should take it or not. I knew it was Ecstasy, but instead of worrying about what it could do to me, I downed it with a double shot of Ciroc, feeling an instant rush. A couple of minutes before it was time for me to start my new career, my conscience kicked in, so I downed three more shots. Finally, I felt high as a kite.

Making my way near the stage, I checked myself out in the full length mirror to make sure I was ready to go. My make-up was good, and I hoped the routine I'd come up with made me a lot of paper tonight. If I was stooping this low to shake my ass for money, then I was going to pull out all stops and make sure that it was worth it. I was ready to shake my ass to the latest Young Jeezy and Jay-Z song in the sexy, bride-to-be outfit that I'd picked out.

My heart was at a fast pace as I held my bouquet tight, and fixed my veil over my face. I was ready to give it all I had. My bright red lipstick stood out, so tonight I was surely going to give a new meaning to a bride draped in pure white. But there was nothing innocent and pure going down over this way.

"Coming to the stage we have a rookie. She a lil' shy so fellas show her some love and give up dat paper. Let's give a good ole' playas welcome to, Miss Ashley," the DJ welcomed me. That was my cue.

"I said I do I do I do I do I do," Jeezy blazed out of the

speakers as I walked up on the stage slow and steady with my cheap, plastic, rhinestone platforms on. I was draped in cheap pearls, but I knew my white sequin dress was going to be the money maker. It was all or nothing.

As I twirled around and dropped it low, I imagined that I was in the privacy of my own home putting on a private show for Diddy. The pill must've started working on me because the more I popped my ass and made my butt cheeks clap, the hornier I got. As I gyrated to the music, the further I felt moisture increase between my legs. Suddenly, I sprang into action and was down to nothing but my pearls in a matter of seconds. The stage was covered with money. Security couldn't get the cash in the bag fast enough before even more flooded the floor. When *Blow the Whistle* by Too Short started pounding through the speakers, that's when I really got busy.

Finally starting to get the hang of it and with the crowd response, my confidence grew. With money on my mind, I spotted this dark skinned dude that was all iced up with all blue on approach the stage. That was my reminder I was in L.A. and he must've been a Crip. Shaking my ass like a maraca, I backed up towards him. Dipping it low and spreading it wide, I shook muscles in my ass that I didn't even know existed. Getting on my back and spreading my legs wide open, my song came on and it was really time to go in on these west coast niggas.

"Bust that pussy open," the dude leaned over between my legs and whispered trying his best to get his feel on.

He continued to drop money all over my body. As I moved the pearls between my legs and played with myself with the beads, he was getting turned on even more by the second. My mission was to suck his pockets dry. Turning over on my knees, I popped my ass some more as he spanked me.

"Yeah, that's right, daddy. Spank this ass, I've been bad," I whispered to him as I made each butt cheek take turns bouncing.

The crowd was going crazy. For my finale, to get my last

hoorah, I broke my pearl necklace and let the pearls splash all over my body. You would've thought I was in the movie, *Flashdance*. The guys loved it as I exited the stage. Even though I was high out of my mind, I was still focused on my money. The entire lawn trash bag was full, I knew I'd hit the jackpot.

As I made my way to the back to count my money, Ray came back there with lust in his eyes.

"Ya sure ya ain't never been on a pole before?" he questioned.

"Oh, I do poles very well," I responded sarcastically.

"Answer da question."

"Never before in public, only behind closed doors. Let me know when you're ready."

"Ya did good for a rookie."

"Rookie huh, so you still calling me rookie? That's cute."

"You are a fuckin' rookie," a deep voice suddenly called out.

It was the girl named Thunder who was big as shit and talked like she had an Adams apple. The only reason why Ray had her there was because she had a donkey booty. Her ass was massive and was 100% natural, so she earned her keep.

"I don't think you were a part of this conversation miss um… who are you again," I shot back, irritated by her red lace bra. That was that same cheap shit my foster mother Tina wore.

"You know my name, bitch," she responded.

"Look, Thunder we don't have time for dat. She did her thang, so ya can't hate," Ray intervened.

"Ray, you defendin' this high yella bitch now? I thought you weren't bringin' no new chicks in here anyway," she barked.

"It's bizness, Thunder! Ya could learn somethin' from rookie," Ray laughed as he smacked me on my ass.

Thunder placed her hands on her wide hips. "I guess she's gonna be your new replacement for Sugar. You likem' high yella anyway."

Before I could turn around to see Ray's reaction, I heard a loud smack. Thunder was on the floor holding her face.

"Why you hit me? All over this rookie!"

"She good peeps, so leave her be. Word to da wise, never mention Sugar again," Ray warned, then turned to me, "Rookie, here go ya earnings," he said in a stern tone handing me a fat envelope before exiting the room.

New to the game, I guess that was how things worked. Just when I thought I was about to get a huge trash bag of bills, the money was decreased in the back. There was no doubt Ray got his cut, but as I counted my bills I was quite pleased.

"Ladies, is this considered a good night, $1500?"

"Bitch, you tryna show off?" Thunder asked with envy.

Her jealousy showed that I was off to a good start. I tried to ignore all the stares, but I just couldn't help myself.

"Leave me be. I'm good peeps," I answered with a smirk.

"Fuck you!" Thunder replied still holding that ugly ass face of hers.

"You're black ass ain't my type," I said, blowing her a kiss.

After putting back on my thong that had a little white train attached along with my dress, I sashayed out of the dressing room. Deciding not to entertain Thunder anymore, I went out into the club to do my meet and greet. At this point I didn't want to give the haters another ounce of energy. It was time for me to make some more cash.

The first table I approached was a table full of street dudes that had bottles of Ace of Spade galore, so I figured they were ballers and it was time to collect some more paper from these bustas. This thirsty bitch shit wasn't my steelo at all, but survival mode kicked in and a girl had to do whatever it took to get back on my game. If anybody back home could see me now they would laugh me out. I had to make sure this was a quick job, no more than a month of this shit.

Putting on a fake sexy smile I approached the table.

"Hey fellas, thanks so much. I see y'all drinking the good shit."

Of course the ugliest of the bunch responded first.

"Where you come from Miss Lady, lookin' all fine and shit? You the baddest thing to come thru here in a longtime."

"Thanks. I'm from down south."

"Where at?"

"Texas," I responded in a dry tone.

He smiled. "What part of Texas? You danced down der, too? I got peeps down der."

I hated the way he talked. "No, tonight was the first night I've ever danced."

"Naw…you fo' real," one of the others blurted out.

I shook my head. "Yeah, no doubt."

"You sound like you from New York or some shit like that. You gotta hell of an accent," the ugly dude said.

I was so busted because that New York accent was something I couldn't shake. Now, I had to backpedal out of this shit so I could get some more bread from their asses.

"I was born in Houston, but we moved to Connecticut when I was like four. Enough about me, what's up with y'all. True West Coast niggas, huh?"

"Straight outta Compton," another one shot out and all but one of them laughed.

Of course the one with the most swag and the dark glasses immediately caught my eye because it seemed like he was the man and all the others were trying to impress him. Once I saw the waitress give him the bill, and he threw a wad full of Ben Franks on the table, I knew he was it. Not trying to seem too thirsty, I played it off like I didn't see him pay the bill and engaged in more conversation with his peons. Laughing with them a little bit I made my way around the table to shake all of their hands, saving the best for last. Once I made it to him and stuck my hand out he didn't respond. Instantly pissed off, I lost it on him.

"What the fuck is your problem?" I blurted out without thinking.

"Yo', who you talkin' to like that, hoe? I'll put a cap in yo' ass for talkin' reckless!" the ugly dude yelled out.

"You were the same ugly motherfucker trying your best to get at me. Now, you acting like you gangster?" I shot back. "You his bodyguard or something? Homie, you don't know me like that."

Instantly, all the dudes got out of their seats like they were all about to attack me at once until the mute motherfucker finally opened his mouth and calmed down his wolf pack.

"Fall back." He raised his hands to his goons and they immediately sat down as he diverted his attention back to me.

"Look, no disrespect, but I don't know where your hands have been, and I'm just not into talking to strippers like that. Y'all cool to look at, but this ain't the South. I'm not trying to wife no stripper let alone hold a conversation with one. Don't get me wrong, I respect your hustle, but I'll never be your meal ticket outta here," he informed.

My mouth was tight. He'd definitely caught me off guard. Back home when I went to the strip club with Sharrod, I turned my nose up at the strippers. Now here I was, one of them. He'd exposed me, but instead of getting mad, it made me want him. I really had something to prove more than ever now. I was up for a challenge. This Scorpio was about to show him that I could have him eating out the palm of my hand. It was hard, but I chose the high road and bowed down.

"Okay, I can respect that" I said and attempted to walk off holding back my tears of anger. But before I could get away, he grabbed my garter and put a big stack of money in it.

"Good luck with your new job, come on, let's bounce," he said as him and his crew cleared out.

The money he gave me did make me feel a little better,

but his words of truth cut like a knife. It hurt and it stung to hear a complete stranger say that, but it was the truth. I didn't even know his name, but I was convinced I would see him again and change his mind about me.

What a night? How do these strippers do this shit every day, I thought to myself a few hours later. I was tired as hell. The money was definitely on point, but having to talk to niggas and fake like I was interested in their lame ass conversation was really not my thing. I was ready to leave, so I decided to head to the dressing room and go home. Mentally I was drained, but physically I was beat. As I walked in the dressing room, it reeked of bleach and I saw all of my shit thrown throughout the entire room.

"Fucking whores!" I belted while gathering my shit.

Everything was completely soaked in bleach. My wardrobe was very limited so for all of my shit to be ruined pissed me off and I was ready to kill a bitch. It was time for war. Making my way to the back of the dressing room ready to fight the first bitch in site, I saw Passion snorting some dope from her compact. Interrupting without a care in the world, I approached her first.

"One question, you touch my shit?"

"What are you talking about, girl? I've been back here getting ready for my set," she replied with white powder on her nose.

"So, who went through my shit?"

"I did, so what are you gonna do about it?"

When I turned around, Thunder stood there while the other three man-looking bitches with her looked like they were ready to attack. But I didn't give a fuck, I wasn't going out like a sucka.

"This is what I'm going to do about it." I grabbed Passion's razor off the counter and headed straight for Thunder's face. She was getting sliced for reminding me of Tina in that lace. All I could see was red.

"Bitch, I'ma kill you!" Thunder shouted as she bent over holding that pothole looking face of hers.

I tried to carve her a new one but just got one slash. There was no way to avoid getting jumped. But if I could get the ringleader, I was satisfied. They were gonna respect me. I was used to bitches trying me until I proved I wasn't a joke. As they stomped and kicked me, I still swung the razor with one hand and landed punches with the other. It was no way I was going to allow them to leave without a gift from me. My ribs felt broken as they finally got me to the floor and stomped me. The taste of blood filled my mouth. It felt like hours of me getting beat down before Ray finally burst through the door.

"Bumbaclot! What da fuck? Get da fuck outta here before I put a cap in all ya bitches. Ya fuckin' up my money. Get them da fuck outta here!" Ray yelled to one of the bouncers.

"Bitch, I'ma see you again," Thunder warned.

Surprisingly, I jumped right up. I'm sure it was from the adrenaline. "Go fuck yourself!" I yelled just before releasing a good wad of spit in Thunder's face.

As Thunder started flipping out, Ray yanked me by my arm and led me all the way to his office. With my body now in pain, I was too angry to cry. I just wanted to fuck somebody up.

"This shit ain't for me, Ray. I can't do this thirsty shit," I said, pacing the room.

"I own ya. You're gonna do what I want ya to," Ray demanded.

"Nigga, you think you own me because you put me up in some ran down ass apartment in the worst part of town? This shit ain't me. I'ma boss bitch and this shit ain't hot. I didn't sign up for all this…"

Before I could finish my sentence Ray smacked me to the floor. I didn't even have time to react before he picked me up by my neck and looked into my eyes. Trying to pull away, I smushed him in his face causing him to hit me again.

"What the fuck did you hit me for?" I yelled.

"Ya think ya so tough. In case ya didn't know, I'm not gainin' shit but a headache by helpin' ya. Ya not givin' me no pussy, so why should I let ya talk shit ta me?"

"So, you want me to fuck you to pay you back? Is that what you want from me? I'm not scared of you, Ray. I don't deserve this shit. What do I have to lose?"

"Ya life! Fuckin' with me, ya lose ya life. So, what's it gonna be? Ya want to be so bad and die behind some bullshit. Ya owe me."

"Owe you for what?" I snapped.

"Savin' ya life, gurl! My brother pick ya up from the bus station and gets hit up for someone tryna take ya head. Now, ya fussin' with Caine and his boys tonight, costin' me money. Me throwin' out Thunder fuckin' up my money, too! Ya see why I own ya now!"

"Stop blaming me for that boy getting shot. I told you…I don't even know anybody out here."

"We don't have beef. So, ya owe me."

"Well, let me pay you back. How much?" I asked.

"All ya got is pennies gurl. Who ya kiddin?" Ray laughed. "Get da fuck out and go home. I'll call ya when I need ya ta cum back."

"No one dismisses me. You want me to fuck you, don't you? I know that you want me. That's why you're so mad."

As Ray ignored me and lit up a blunt, anger filled my veins. I hated his ass for what he was saying to me, but he was all I had at the moment. I had to get back on his good side, and it killed me to put my pride aside. I didn't need my money to get fucked up over some bullshit.

"You sure you don't want this?" I asked, opening my legs trying to turn him on.

"I don't want ya Ashley, ya not my type. Now, go

home."

"You just don't know how good this pussy is. Look how pink it is."

Trying to entice him with all I had still didn't work. What he said next made me feel worthless. I wasn't used to being rejected.

"Ashley, I don't want a reckless bitch in my bed. Now, go find a bottom nigga to fuck and get out of my office."

Kennedi-10

"Bitch, you're gonna die!" I heard just before hanging up.

Someone called my phone from a private number at least twice a week threatening my life. With the voice so distorted, I didn't know who it was and was tired of their harassment. Now that I had enough money to get a new phone, it was definitely top priority.

It was probably Sharrod's miserable ass, but this shit had to stop. A part of me was starting to believe Ray was right. Maybe somebody was trying to get at me. I turned over and put my head under the covers, trying to take another power nap before it was time for me to get up for work. Since I normally didn't get home until five a.m. every night, getting enough rest so I could perform well had been my routine for the past couple of weeks. Today for some reason, however, was hard as hell to get out of bed. I was never a 9-5 type of chick, and up until now had never worked a day in my life. That was one thing Sharrod was good for. The fact that he took care of me for so long had truly been a gift.

Realizing that I couldn't rest, I grabbed my newest US Weekly magazine to see what was going on in the lives of the rich and famous. There was so much drama and divorce going on it didn't make much sense. From Heidi Klum and Seal, to Tom Cruise and Katie, as well as all of the new Kardashian drama; everyone was calling it quits.

As I read the latest celebrity dish, I tore out some of the

hottest fashions to add to my wish board that hung on my closet door. My dream was to be in the, '*who wore it best'* segment and kill the scene with my fly swag. There was nothing that was gonna stop me from getting back on my game, where red bottoms was all I rocked. Now, buying a pair of Uggs was a luxury for me. As the old saying goes, *you can go from sugar to shit in a blink of an eye.* I was definitely a prime example of that. Although the money I made at the club was pretty good, I still just wanted to find the right dude so I could chill, sit back, and look pretty.

In the meantime, before my come up came to light, I made it my business to make a couple of connections at the club to try and get into modeling or videos. It was just a matter of time before something was gonna come through. Men were marks and I knew that L.A. had been the right move. My day was coming and I would soon have the fame and the fortune. There was no way I was gonna settle.

My situation has to get better, I thought after getting out of bed and heading straight for the shower. It was already after seven p.m.

It was frustrating as hell to have to take a shower in this hell hole. It made me feel like I was back in jail. If I was going to be on the streets I needed to live like it. Jacuzzi bubble baths was my calm at night and my joy in the morning. Having to get a gym membership was annoying in itself. I was used to being able to go downstairs in my basement and work out. Something had to give.

Making my way to the bathroom I turned on the water. It was ice cold.

"What the fuck?" I yelled.

I couldn't believe Ray's bitch ass obviously hadn't paid the gas bill. As I walked to the kitchen to confirm, just as I thought, the stove wouldn't turn on. Immediately, I grabbed my cell phone to curse his ass out, but before I could dial his number my phone rang with an unknown number.

At first I wasn't going to answer it because I was tired of the constant arguments with Sharrod. Then I thought about it and felt it could be someone calling about a modeling gig. This was the only phone I had at the moment and there was no bill, so having to deal with Sharrod was something minor. Not in the mood for his shit, I answered the phone ready for war.

"What does your punk ass want now?"

"Mommy?"

I paused for a second. "Chase, is that you?"

"Mommy, when are you coming home? I miss you."

"Chase, where are you? How did you get this number?"

"My daddy gave it to me. Big Mama dialed it for me."

I shook my head. "Where is Big Mama?"

"Her right here."

"Let me speak to her ass."

I could hear some whispering before my grandmother got on the phone.

"Well, hello Kennedi. So glad you finally decided to answer," she said.

"Why the hell did you call me for Chase? Who asked you to do that?"

"Is that how you greet someone?" she replied, offending the fuck out of me. "And Sharrod asked me to," she continued. "He's concerned and wanted me to talk some sense into you. What on Earth made you think it was okay for you to just run off to Los Angeles without telling anyone? You left your son behind while you chase after some money. Is that more important to you than this boy?" she slurred. Her speech was a little impaired from her last stroke.

"Well, I hope you're not calling me about money because if it is, then you better ask Sharrod. Oh, I forgot, he's in prison." I snickered. "He wanted Chase remember…not me. Now, you're probably gonna blame me because his fat ass is not out to take care of him."

"Chile, I don't need a dime from you. Sharrod has been

taking care of this boy the entire two years you were locked up. He still doesn't want for anything but his mama. It's been two years since you've seen Chase. You ought ta be ashamed of yourself. Every Sunday I pray that God will find a way in your spirit. Lord knows I didn't raise you to be this way."

"Raise me? You took care of me a couple of years and you want some credit?"

"Chile, you must've lost your God forsaken mind if you think I'm gonna stand for your disrespect. Your son wanted to talk to you. He's falling behind in school and has been withdrawn lately. He's yearning for you and all you can think about is yourself."

"Big Mama, let me see the phone!" I could hear my twin sister Kasey yelling in the background.

"Hello!" she yelled in the phone seconds later.

"What?" I answered.

"Don't be upsetting my grandmother like that! You know I should come to L.A. and whoop your trifling ass for leaving Chase. Do you know how much he cries for you?"

"Bring your ass out here and watch what I do."

Kasey knew I never minded beating her ass. The last time she got it from me was when I caught her all leaned up in Sharrod's truck when we first started messing with each other.

"All you do is send threats, Kennedi. You don't appreciate anything. Sharrod was good to you and you did him wrong. You fuck his best friend, you leave his son…"

"Kasey, who's side are you on?" I interrupted.

"Not yours," she shot back.

"That's nothing new. Just like old times. You never had my back and that's why your luck is so fucked up 'til this day. You still ain't landed a baller to save you from that hell hole. You always wanted to be me. Now, you can have Sharrod, sweetie. Play house with his son since that's the life you wanted so bad."

"Kennedi, Big Mama is sick. You can't expect her to

raise Chase."

"I know you ain't talking. You leave your son with her all the time, with his little gay ass."

"With all the skeletons and secrets you got I know you better shut your damn mouth. If I blew up your spot I could fuck up your whole life. You're lucky I care about her," Kasey replied.

"You care about who?"

"Oh, you know who the hell I'm talking about, now try me."

"Get off my phone talking reckless, you jealous slut!" I belted.

"Mark my word, your luck is gonna run out. Trust me…all secrets come to the light. And for the record, I'm tired of you calling me jealous."

"Well, it's the truth. You've been jealous of me since forever."

"That's right, switch the subject as usual. Hide from all those skeletons. It makes me sick that I share the same face as you. Don't you have a conscience? Your son is sitting here crying his eyes out because he wants his mother," Kasey responded. "Guess I'll continue to pick up your slack like I have for the past two years while your ass was in prison. I'll make sure my nephew grows up to be somebody. Sharrod don't want you and Chase doesn't need you anyway."

"Boo-Boo, you'll never be me. Fuck you, fuck Sharrod, fuck Big Mama, and fuck Chase's soft ass, too. I'm not gonna battle you to be his mother."

"When you don't do right by your kids, you'll never have good luck. Mark my words," Kasey warned.

"I want my Mommy. Oooohhhh, I want my Mommy!" Chase yelled and screamed in the background.

Kasey sucked her teeth. "See what you've done, and what we have to deal with."

"Y'all called me. Who the fuck wants to deal with that

crying and shit? Y'all making that little boy a sissy, just like your son. Man, get the fuck off my phone. As a matter of fact, I'll have a new one soon so this shit can't keep happening," I spat.

"You're just like her and don't even see it."

"Like who, I ain't nothing like these chicks out here. I'm in a league of my own."

"No, you're just like Mona. Her blood runs real good in your veins."

My eyes increased. Now, I was beyond furious. "Fuck you, Kasey! I'm nothing like her!" I yelled after hanging up the phone.

Kasey had definitely struck a chord when she thought it was okay to compare me to my dead beat ass mother. My blood boiled and my mind filled with mixed emotions. I always hated Kasey. There was a lot I had to hide and if she ever thought about letting my secrets out it really could destroy me. She'd really crossed the line this time by bringing that shit up. Now, not caring about the water being cold, I got in the shower mad as hell and in deep thought. My day had to get better.

After getting out of the shower a few minutes later, I went to my closet to get dressed and pack my bag for work. Dancing had afforded me to buy a few pieces to get my wardrobe together, but even more importantly it afforded me to buy a little black 2003 Volkswagen Beetle. It wasn't the Porsche Panamera that I wanted, but it would work for now. A couple of weeks of dancing had gotten me on my knees crawling, but I couldn't wait to get back on my feet running in full force.

Since Ray had me doing private dances most of the time, now I was making more money and good connections were definitely coming to light. I even started investing in my own custom made costumes to step up my game. I especially loved the sexy new Lakers outfit, and couldn't wait to wear it. It was metallic gold with purple rhinestones all over it. Since the Lakers had a home game tonight, not only were we gonna be super busy, but I was gonna make major paper once I put it on. Tonight was gonna be my night. I was determined not to let my family bring my spirits down even more than they already were.

Since I got up late, I didn't have time to go to the gym or get my hair done, so wet and wavy was the way I had to go. Big hair got me more tips anyway. After quickly getting dressed and hopping in my car, I got to work in less than twenty minutes. The club was packed already.

"Hey, chica," Isis said, greeting me.

"What's up, Ice?"

"I was given strict orders that when you came in you were to go straight to see Ray."

"I need to see that nigga anyway. What kind of mood is he in?" I inquired.

"Shitty. What mood do you think he's in?" Isis replied with a huge grin.

"Well, knowing him he's watching the camera and knows I'm here already. See you later."

"Looking cute, too. Those jeans hugging that phat ass."

"Girl, whatever."

Ignoring Isis' flirtatious comments, I made my way to Ray's office. He was already on my shit list anyway for not paying the gas bill. Once I got to the backdoor, I could hear him on the phone laughing so I figured he was in a good mood.

"Here she is right here," Ray said, passing me the phone. I had no idea who it was. "Hello."

"I hear you out there giving my pussy away."

A smile instantly invaded my face. "What's up? I miss you."

"How can you miss me? I ain't heard from you since you been in L.A.," Shawn replied.

"It ain't like I can call you."

"Don't get out there and get cute now. You know you in my territory."

"Girl, shut up. What's been up? When you coming home?"

"Same ole shit. But you're not gonna believe that I got another two years for shanking this chick in here."

"Are you serious?' I asked upset. "Why would you do something like that?"

"Because she was talking shit, that's why, and you know how I roll," Shawn informed. "But it's cool though, no worries. I'll be alright. You know I got a new cellie."

"Oh yeah," I said a little jealous. There was so much I wanted to say, but couldn't with Ray staring down my throat.

"She not as good as you so don't be mad."

"I know that."

"I wish I could taste that pussy right now."

"Me too," I said being short.

Shawn laughed. "I guess Ray fucking up our moment right now, huh? I know you got so much to say."

"I sure do."

"You better not fuck him either."

"Girl, please. Not interested at all."

"You know I got eyes all over. That's my town, so don't try to get cute," Shawn advised.

"Never that."

"That pussy wet, ain't it?"

"Stop, dammit!" I yelled. I couldn't take it anymore because I was wet. She was a beast and I needed one of those orgasms right about now.

"So, are you gonna give me your cell number? All this time I didn't think you had a phone yet until Ray said he was gonna call to see how far away you were."

"What do you mean? You got me the phone when I left. It was in my package."

"How the hell was I gonna get you a phone?" Shawn asked.

I was beyond confused. "So, where the hell did the

phone come from?"

Before I could get an answer the phone hung up. My heart dropped to my stomach. Sharrod's name was written all over it. Now, I knew C.O. Bates had planted the phone in my bag.

Maybe Sharrod really was the one who had me shot at that day, I thought. Ray was right, someone was after me, and that someone was probably Sharrod.

"What da hell is wrong with ya gurl?" Ray questioned.

"Why the hell didn't you pay the gas bill? I had to take a cold ass shower," I said, skipping the subject.

"If ya got money to pierce ya tongue, nipples, and pussy, then ya got money to pay ya own bills. Ya already live rent free."

"That's all you had to say. All you had to do was tell me."

Ray lifted his hand like a strict parent. "Ya want me to smack ya down again? Stop ya smart back talk."

"Nigga, you need some good pussy in your life so you won't be so damn mad all the time."

Before he could respond Isis walked in.

"Okay Ray, so I have some good news and some bad news," she stated.

"Spill it."

"The good news is Malcolm Fitzgerald just came in, so somebody is about to get paid. The bad news is, he's with those blood niggas."

"Yo', he brought Bloods in my spot. Why da fuck would he bring Bloods into Crip territory? Tell him he gotta go to a private room. I'll be on the camera so I can make sure there are no problems." He looked at me. "Get dressed, Ashley. I need ya to go give him a private dance. He's got mad money."

"Bet," I said, leaving out the door with a huge smile. I was lucky to be chosen. It was time to make this dance really count. I had nothing to lose.

Kennedi-11

After getting dressed, I walked out of the dressing room laughing at all the dirty looks. These whores looked like they wanted to kill me, and I didn't even know who this Malcolm dude were. Once I got to room number eight where Malcolm and his crew was, I couldn't wait to see who this dude was that had the girls beefing with me. As soon as I walked in, I was blinded by greatness. This had to be the most handsome dude in L.A.

"Well, good evening, Miss Lady," he flirted.

As fine as he was, I didn't mind. "How are you?"

"Even better now. So, you're a Laker's fan, huh?"

"Huge fan," I lied.

"A beautiful fan I might add."

I blushed.

He had four other dudes with him and one of them was Neko Luv, the rapper I'd just seen on 106 & Park the other day. The young girls were on the show going crazy over him, but he wasn't my type. He was cute and all, but you could tell he was rapped up in that gang shit. Turned me straight off with his all red. Malcolm, on the other hand, was drop dead gorgeous. He was way over six feet tall so you could easily mistake him for a basketball player. He even looked like he could've been Indian or Dominican with his reddish brown skin tone and his coal black wavy hair. With perfect teeth and a sexy smile to match, it looked like he'd stepped straight out of a magazine.

Usually, I didn't get caught up in how the guys looked

who came in the club, but this nigga was different. Any other time I just saw dollar signs, but Malcolm could definitely be a prospect. I hadn't had a real nigga in my adult life, so I was due for some good dick and arm candy. A girl like me fantasized over dudes like him all day long while I was locked up playing with myself.

As soon as I was ready for action, the Lakers won the game against the Celtics. Being an East Coaster, I was pissed. Not wasting any time; as soon as *Get Your Money Up* by Keri Hilson came on, I instantly went into instant freak mode. I didn't pay any of the others guys any attention. My focus was to turn him out.

"Damn, baby you gonna show us some love over here," one of the guys blurted out.

"You'll get your turn," I lied as I gyrated in Malcolm's face before getting on his lap.

"You a sexy lil' thing."

"You haven't seen nothing yet," I hissed sexily.

Before I knew it, my body was slithering like a snake and Malcolm's eyes enlarged to the fullest.

"Damnnnnn," Malcolm exhaled.

Money flew everywhere. Fuck making it rain, it was a damn tsunami in that room. Making my way over to the others, I shook my ass like I needed a new Benz. They were going crazy.

"Now, this is a real chick right here!" Malcolm commented.

"You thinking what I'm thinking," one of the others replied back.

"Are y'all talking about me?" I stopped dancing and made my way to the couch.

There had to be over $3,000 on the floor, so I definitely needed a trash bag. My garter definitely wouldn't hold the amount of cash that filled the room. Only twenty's and above, no George Washington's were in sight.

"Well, Miss Lady…"

"Ashley. My name is Ashley," I politely interrupted Malcolm.

"Is that your real name?"

I nodded. "Yes."

"How long you been dancing?"

"A couple of weeks, why?"

"Usually dancers don't give up their governments," one of the other dudes chimed in.

"Oh well, now you know, I'm Ashley, one of the realest chicks you gonna meet in your life," I said, staring at my future husband.

"Well, we're working on a project and you have the look we're looking for. It would be the perfect come up for you. Wouldn't you love to retire from…"

Before Malcolm could complete his sentence, Ray barged into the room. With me sitting on the couch instead of shaking my ass, I knew it was going to be a problem.

"A still body don't get fed. What ya' sittin' for, Ashley?" Ray asked.

My heart dropped once Ray stormed in. I prayed to God he hadn't heard what Malcolm said.

"What's up Ray, it's my fault," Malcolm defended.

"In my office, Ashley. Now!" Ray yelled.

"Can I get my money first?" I asked.

Ray shook his head. "Butch will get it."

I shook mine as well. "Oh, hell no. I'm getting my own money. He's not gonna…"

At that moment, Ray picked me up and carried me out of the room before I could even try to stand my ground. I was so humiliated. Any chance of getting Malcolm was more than likely ruined. It felt like my overprotective father had just caught me in bed with somebody and I was about to get a spanking.

"What the fuck is your problem?" I yelled as soon as we

got into his office.

"You, bitch!"

"What?"

"This what happens to disrespectful bitches!"

"Nigga, I was getting money!"

Smack, smack, smack...

Ray continuously hit me until I was on the poorly car-peted floor. My face stung. I could feel the whelps instantly rise up on my face. There was no way he was gonna think it was okay to keep putting his hands on me. Standing up, I swung and punched him right in his face. Any object that was on his desk I threw at him as he came at me. Glass shattered everywhere when the ashtray I hurled at him caused his Bob Marley Paint-ing to fall to the floor.

By the time Butch came in with the trash bag, my nails were deeply embedded into Ray's face. As soon as Butch sepa-rated us, Ray went straight to his drawer. I knew what that meant. Out of breath, we both panted with anger filled eyes as Ray aimed his .32 caliber at me.

"Ya bumbaclot bitch! I kill ya!"

"Do it!" I said, daring him.

"No, man, no. Y'all trippin'. Y'all lucky nobody heard y'all in here. Ray you know cops are always out there cuz of these crazy ass gang members so chill," Butch interjected shielding me.

"Move Butch!" Ray roared.

"No. You not gonna lose everything over some dumb shit," Butch responded.

"Get da fuck outta my club," Ray said, waving his gun.

"Fuck you, Ray. I'll be out of your shit tonight. Crazy motherfucker. Who the fuck beats on women, you pussy ass nigga!" I yelled in return. "Butch, give me my money!"

"That's my money. You bit off the hand that fed ya," Ray demanded.

"Give me my fucking money!" I snatched the bag from

Butch and backed out the room.

"Just let her go," I heard Ray say as I made my way straight to the dressing room.

By the time I got to my locker and started pulling stuff out, Isis came in the back being nosey.

"What the fuck happened?"

"Your boy tripping, so I'm out."

"Well, that's nothing new," Isis replied. "If you need a place to stay, just call me."

"Alright," I said, blowing her off. I just wanted to get my shit and leave.

As soon as I got outside, Thunder and her girls were all out front waiting for me. I definitely wasn't in the mood for this shit. Malcolm and his boys were leaving out and I didn't know if I should try and walk out with them or go out there by myself. Just my luck one of the police officers that frequented the club, came outside to smoke a cigarette.

"Hey, Thunder," I called out with a sneaky grin.

"You lucky. I'ma get your ass."

I grinned. "Next time, babe."

"Oh, there'll be a next time, for sure, bitch!"

I blew a kiss at her and got in my car. Just as I started the engine, I looked up to see Malcolm at my car door. He scared the hell out of me.

"Boy, you scared me!"

"What the hell happened to your face?" he questioned.

"I just got fired. I guess you can see how Ray wasn't too happy with me talking to you guys."

He seemed shocked. "So, he hit you. Are you kidding me?"

"Look, I'm quite humiliated right now and I'm trying to figure out where I'm gonna lay my head tonight so I really need to go."

"Where do you stay?"

"No where now," I responded.

"What do you mean?"

"Well, I had just moved out here about a month ago and Ray was letting me stay in one of his apartments. Now, I have nowhere to go."

"Damn, I feel responsible, I'm sorry. The project I was telling you about. You got the job. That's my way to repay you."

"I'm sorry. After all the shit I just went through, I can't remember everything you said. What kind of project?"

Malcolm grinned. "A reality show I'm producing."

"Ummmmm, I don't know about that."

"Just give it some thought," he told me with a grin.

"Get in. I know your neck hurts from leaning over in the window," I said, trying to be humorous since he was so tall. He looked funny trying to bend over into my little Beetle.

As soon as Malcolm motioned to his boys that he was good, I unlocked my door and he climbed inside. He could barely fit, but after adjusting the seat, we were able to engage in a conversation for almost an hour. I told him so many lies about my life that I hoped I would be able to keep up. There was no way I was mentioning anything about being down for two years, or Chase. His little ass could ruin my chances.

Malcolm was so well educated and so opposite of what I was used to that I was a little uncomfortable. It felt like if my grammar wasn't on point he would immediately be turned off.

We had an instant connection and I felt a way with him that I'd never felt before. I couldn't figure out if I was just vulnerable or needed a knight in shining armor? At this point I needed to be saved, and Malcolm made me feel safe. Not to mention, he was damn sure good to look at. Suddenly, he put his hand on my thigh, which I didn't mind. Just when he leaned over to try and steal a kiss, bright lights flashed from everywhere.

"What the hell?" I asked looking around.

"Fucking paparazzi. Man, do y'all ever sleep?" Malcolm

yelled. "Sweetheart, follow me, we gotta bounce. I'll make sure you alright."

"Are you serious? What the fuck are those people taking pictures for?" I yelled as he got out and ran to his car.

Moments later, Malcolm took off as if he'd gotten caught in the rain and needed shelter. Just when I thought today couldn't get any worse, Malcolm made me feel like I'd just been rescued from the devil. I took him up on his offer and pulled off behind his car with nothing to lose. If the paparazzi were taking pictures then I knew my life could get nothing but better with Malcolm in it.

Kennedi-12

"So, this is my bachelor pad," Malcolm said as we walked into his marble foyer.

"Wow, it's beautiful." I was in awe. Everything in L.A. just looked much more luxurious than anything on the East Coast. I loved it out here.

It was a little embarrassing that I still was dressed in my Lakers costume, so grabbing something to eat was out of the question. But I didn't expect for Malcolm to bring me to his penthouse. He was very respectful and gentle, which was something I just wasn't used to.

"You live here alone?" I picked up a picture of a cute little girl with long hair that looked just like him. Lord knows I didn't have the patience for no crumb snatchers. I didn't even want my own.

"Yeah. My daughter comes through sometimes, but this is my spot by myself."

"You don't have no baby mama drama, do you?"

"Naw, babe. I try to stay drama free. Come have a seat, I don't bite," Malcolm replied.

Nervous about making the wrong move, I was still in the foyer while he was already sitting down on the big white sofa. He made me feel like I had to be perfect for some reason. From his perfect appearance to his spotless home, it felt like I was out of my league. The pit of my stomach filled with butterflies. Instantly, I felt uneasy with the fear of it being obvious that I needed a come up.

"Oh, sorry."

"What you so nervous about? Damn, your eye is getting worse. Let me see if I got some ice."

"I heard steak helps," I said before we both laughed. "I hate Ray for doing this to me."

My face felt like it had a pulse. Pain filled my head. I was so embarrassed.

"Is he your man or something?" Malcolm questioned.

"Hell no. He's not my type," I answered with disgust.

"Well, what's your type?"

"You."

"That's nice to know!" he yelled back from the kitchen.

As I looked around there were pictures of Malcolm on different magazine covers on the walls, but my favorite was the GQ shirtless photo. There were also professional photos of his daughter everywhere. She looked like a model. I guess she came with the package. Hopefully there was a way of avoiding that part of his life and still be his girl.

"So, how is your relationship with your daughter's mother?" I was curious about that part.

"To be honest, we're off and on. Right now, we're off. She has a hard time dealing with my lifestyle, and I don't do well with nagging."

Note to self, I whispered under my breath.

"What's your lifestyle? What do you do Mr. Malcolm?" He smiled. "A lot of things."

"So, you like Tommy on *Martin,* huh?"

"You really don't know who I am, huh?" he inquired.

"Am I supposed to know?"

"Well, I don't see why you don't. I'm Malcolm Fitzgerald, an entrepreneur and deeply involved in the world of entertainment."

I could hear the sounds of a cash register in my head.

"Enough about me, do you have baby daddy drama?"

"No kids. Just me, myself, and I. Gotta keep this body

tight as long as I can," I lied

"Oh really. Why not? Do you want kids someday?"

"I want to do things right. I want the white picket fence life, one day. No time soon, though. I need to get me together, first," I said, assuring him that there was no need to run.

"I can dig it, and to be honest, I can help get you on your feet quicker than you think, and definitely quicker than that nigga Ray."

"Oh, really. So, the project you had in mind for me, tell me about it."

"Well, my partner and I are piloting a reality show and I thought you had the look we were going for."

"Why me?"

"Why not? You're beautiful and I think this is what you need to escape Ray's world. Do you sing?"

"In the shower. I can rap a little though." I laughed embarrassed.

"That helps," he said, licking his sexy thick lips.

Malcolm was right. The hell with Ray and his club! The only thing I needed from that bastard was the money I'd stashed in his apartment. It was my time to shine. I was willing to do anything at this point to get in Malcolm's good graces.

As the minutes passed, he went on and on to tell me about his vision for the show. The downside was I had to compete for this dude's love that I could care less about. Of course, I wondered if the show would hurt my chances of being with Malcolm. The good thing was, he assured me that fame and opportunity would come knocking. All those reality chicks were getting paid, but to be honest I was ready to chill, for sure I was already tired of working hard, and being Malcom's arm candy was the end goal. Wifey status was in my future and I could be back to the lifestyle I knew best. At this point, I had nothing to lose. Now, was a pivotal moment for me. Another wrong move could send me to a new state trying to find a meal ticket.

"It's cool to know that I would be the winner at the end,

but I'm still on the fence about it," I stated.

"Well, we're way behind on production. Time is money. I'm known for creating stars. All you have to do is just fake like you like the dude. You know Neko Luv, right?"

"Of course. I saw him with you tonight."

"He's gonna be the star of the show," Malcolm informed. "There's something special about you. If you trust me, you'll always be straight. I can change your life. I told you that you're guaranteed to come out of the competition on top. Do you know how many doors that will open for you?" He sounded like a car salesman trying to make a quota.

"Okay, I'm in. You've convinced me. I'm in," I said, hugging him.

His eyes lit up with excitement. "Miss Ashley, you've just picked the winning lottery ticket. Your life is about to change. Now, are you ready for the fame, some can't handle it?"

"I have absolutely nothing to lose," I responded with my arms still draped around his neck. He smelled so damn good.

Malcolm stared deep into my eyes. "Anything you need, I got you," he whispered.

Embarrassed with my appearance, I pulled away. "Well, for starters, I feel so uncomfortable in this costume. I wish I had some clothes to change into. Your house just makes me feel so funny dressed like this."

"You can be yourself with me. I'm not gonna judge you."

"Well, do you have a t-shirt or something I could put on?"

"I like the Lakers thing you got going on, but if you want a t-shirt, that can be arranged."

As soon as Malcolm got up to go upstairs, we both heard keys at the door. He looked nervous as hell as the door opened seconds later. He looked like he'd just seen a ghost as she walked in. His guest surprised the hell out of me, too.

"Hey, Malcolm, what's this all about?"

"Umm, I didn't know you were coming over, Isis," he mumbled.

"You told me to hit you when I got off and I've been calling you ever since. I figured you just wanted me to meet you over here. Ashley, what are you doing here?" she said, dropping her overnight bag on the floor irritated.

"Don't answer that, Ashley. What the fuck I need to ask you is how you got my damn keys and how you got into the gate?" Malcolm questioned.

Isis placed her hands on her hips. "The same place I always get them from, under the flowerpot in the hall. Why the twenty million questions? If I came at a bad time, just let me know."

"Ashley had a rough night thanks to your friend, Ray so yeah you came at a bad time."

I was still in shock as the two of them went back and forth.

"So, what is wifey gonna think about you sleeping with another stripper Malcolm?" Isis asked.

My eyes widened. *Wife*, I thought. This nigga was lying already.

"Isis, give me my keys, you need to go," Malcolm said, keeping his cool.

"Well, me and Ashley know each other very well. I'm sure she won't mind if I stay. A party of three has never stopped us before."

If Isis let Malcolm in on anything about us, I was gonna beat her ass. I didn't need her fucking up my chances.

"Isis, I'll call you tomorrow. It's not that type of party. I just needed some place to stay tonight," I spoke up.

"Well, you can stay at my place. Ashley, he's married with a daughter," Isis continued to snitch.

"No, she's good here. Now, you need to leave," Malcolm said, ignoring her comment.

"I know your whole rap sheet, Malcolm. I never wanted you to wife me, just loved the big dick, that's all. Fucking you from time to time had its perks. Ashley, how you gonna get him to wife you? Many have tried."

Feeling like she was underestimating what I was capable of, I fell for the bait. "I'd have to charge you if I let you know. See, if you were that bitch, then you wouldn't be leaving right now, I would. If he's married then evidently wifey ain't playing her position. That's when I come in, and make everything in Malcolm's life all better."

It was funny as I watched her deflate. Isis really didn't know me, because I didn't give a fuck about a baby mother, a wife, or a jump off. Malcolm was gonna be my ticket to the top. It was a must that I pulled out all the stops to have him just like I had Sharrod.

"You think it's that easy?" Isis asked with a little smirk.

"I know it is," I quickly shot back.

Malcolm started clapping his hands. "Okay, okay ladies. Isis, you gotta go before I call security."

"Malcolm, go to hell, and lose my number!" Isis yelled throwing his keys at him, right before slamming the door.

Silence fell over the room for a few seconds before he finally cleared his throat.

"Well, I apologize for that. Umm…"

Before he could even explain, I just kissed him. There was no need for an explanation. As bad as I wanted to save myself and not have sex with him right away, I had to turn him out. Plan B had to go into effect. He was my only savior right now. If he had a wife at this point, I really didn't care.

"Hold up I need to tell…" he tried to say.

"Don't tell me anything, just kiss me."

His lips felt so soft, and his cologne smelled so clean, which made me want him even more. As I rubbed my hands on his soft hair, I found myself sitting on his lap, stuck in a pasionate long kiss.

"Malcolm, take my clothes off."

"I don't think we should do this," he said in between pants.

"I want you, Malcolm."

"But I don't have any condoms, do you?"

"Malcolm, I haven't had sex with a man in over two years, I'm safe."

He looked at me like I was crazy. "Are you serious?"

"Yes, now stop talking and take care of me."

He did just that. He caressed my body and kissed me all over my neck so gentle. He was just what I needed. He was my knight tonight that was soon to be my king. Getting off his lap and getting on my knees, I sucked his pole as if he was my favorite cherry popsicle. The size of Malcolm made me nervous. He was huge. I knew he was going to split my juicy box wide open.

"Feel me Malcolm, I'm so wet," I said, placing his hand between my legs.

"Damn, you are. Let's take this to my bedroom."

I didn't even have time to look around his room because we couldn't stop kissing. As Malcolm carried me to the bed, he laid me down and removed all my clothes. As soon as he took everything off, I just stared at him in disbelief. He was too perfect.

"This ain't right. I can't do nothing without a condom," he said.

Not in the mood for rejection, a thought quickly popped in my head. *If we get in the shower or bathtub together I can work my mojo.*

"Okay, I understand. I need to take a bath anyway. Can you run me some bath water?"

"Sure. You definitely need to soak in the Jacuzzi after the night you had. I'm gonna hook you up."

He damn sure did. He had candles lit up and some more shit. As I got in the bubble bath, I was so happy that I started crying. Since I'd been home, all I wanted to do was take a bath.

"What's wrong?"

"Nothing. I just have a lot on my mind."

"Just relax," Malcolm said as he washed my back with a sponge.

"Can you get in with me?"

"Of course."

That big pole was at attention again and I knew once I had him in the tub it was curtains. If there was any nigga that I would've let knock me up, Malcolm was it. He had legit money. Even though I didn't fuck with kids like that, he had that millionaire money. He was in a league I was trying to get in.

As soon as he got in the Jacuzzi, I went under water as if I was snorkeling and started sucking his dick making sure he had a good visual of my ass poking out.

"Ahh, ahh Ashley, damn."

"You like it?" I asked coming up for air.

"I love it," he moaned.

With his manhood continuously jerking, I knew it was almost time for him to cum, and it was time for me to make it count. It was now or never. Sucking and slurping, finally, I came out from under the water and started trying to sit on his lap. But I was so tight, he wouldn't fit. With the water making me even tighter, it didn't help.

"Man, fuck this, come on," Malcolm stated.

Carrying me out of the tub, we tracked water all on his marble floors until we were on the bed. Not wasting much time, he spread both of my legs open and tried to enter me again. It hurt like hell.

"Damn, you were telling the truth, huh?"

"Ouch…shit."

"You want me to stop?"

"No, I want you."

After a few more attempts, his big pole was finally able to thrust deep inside of me and it felt so damn good. The way

he looked at me and stroked in and out was different than anything I'd ever felt before. There was no doubt he was the one. I
was willing to do whatever it took to keep him. It was time for
me to get back on my game and fuck his brains out; even if it
hurt like hell. This was my one shot to show him I was all he
needed.

"Let me get on top," I suggested.

"Okay."

Climbing on top of him, I placed a couple of pillows by
the arch of his back. Now, he was in the right position as I
worked him back inside of me making every stroke count.

"Grab my ass baby, grab it," I ordered.

Malcolm complied as I tightened my lips. Wishes that he
would only want to be in my warm pussy forever flooded my
mind. It was my mission tonight to make him want only me.

"Shit, Ashley I'm about to cum!"

"Don't cum yet, please. I want you to keep fucking me,
please don't come."

"No, move!"

"Please don't cum. Please don't stop, it feels too good."

"Shit, I'm cumming, fuck!"

"Don't cum in me, Malcolm!"

"It's too late…fuck!"

Mission accomplished.

Malcolm-13

"Thanks for breakfast this morning," I whispered to Ashley while she was in between filming, which gave me the perfect opportunity to flirt.

"Anything for my man," she whispered into my ear.

I gave off a quick undercover grin. "Sexy ass self," I mouthed softly.

She reached to rub my leg, but I backed away, hoping no one saw her attempt.

"She's been missing you," Ashley mumbled, while pointing to her clit.

"Soon. Very soon," I muttered back.

Our relationship was strictly on the low for several reasons. On top of me not wanting people all in my business, I needed to keep Ashley happy for the show to be successful. With Ashley being the guaranteed winner in the end, we had to at least fake as if she was somewhat interested in Neko Luv. This was our third week of filming, and I was excited at the amount of press Ashley was receiving. All the girls hated her already, and they stayed at each other's throats. The only frustrating thing was seeing Neko Luv all over my new chick, but since the show was creating so much buzz, I was cool with it. I had big plans for her, and with money on the line, there was no room for error.

What have I gotten myself into, I thought eying my newest project.

For the past month, I hadn't been home. Ashley really

had me stuck on stupid, and damn near had me under the covers
sucking my thumb like a fucking baby. It wasn't just the fact
that she was a born again virgin and had the tightest, wettest
pussy that I'd ever entered in my life, but her head game was
enough in itself to keep me occupied these past couple of
weeks. I didn't even feel bad anymore about not strapping up
the first time we had sex or bringing a complete stranger to my
crib. Ashley was different. It was something about her that
made me feel needed. Things were moving fast and for the first
time I was okay with my whirlwind life.

The reality show was being filmed at a mansion in Beverly Hills. We definitely brought the hood to the Hills. It was already action packed with lots of hair pulling and drama. My
only concern was making sure that Ashley remained the high-
light of the show to open endorsement deals and much more in
the future. She was my new investment that was gonna make
me a lot of money.

"Can I borrow this beautiful lady for a second," I interrupted, as Ashley finished up her last interview for the day. She
was even more beautiful once hair and make-up dolled her up.
We snuck off to a private room away from the cameras.

"Malcolm, thank you so much for this opportunity. I'm
forever grateful to you. I mean, they're treating me like a superstar already," Ashley stated with a massive grin.

"Get used to it. This is just the beginning, babe. Look at
you. You're gorgeous."

"You did this. Malcolm, you saved my life." She felt exactly how I wanted her to.

"Well, what do you want to do next after this, because I
can make it happen? You're such a natural in front of the camera."

"Who knows? I'm twenty-four, single, and open to anything. L.A. has been good to me so far."

"So, what made you move out here anyway? I mean I
know you told me you were into fashion, but what made you go

the dancer route."

"Don't say it, Malcolm. You keep telling me I'm too pretty to be a dancer. I heard you. I feel everyone has a guardian angel and you're mine. You came into my life at just the right time. Don't get me wrong, I'm not looking for a ring or anything, but I enjoy hanging out with you. I mean, I…"

I lifted up my index finger to stop her. "You don't have to say anything else. We're going to come up with a plan for you to take this city by storm," I said, before giving her a gentle kiss on her forehead and then straight to her full, pink lips.

Ashley turned her head slightly. "Hold up."

"What…I can't kiss you?"

"You can do more than that," she replied. "I just want you to know I'm serious. I appreciate you."

There was innocence about her that turned me on. It was like she needed me to let her know everything was gonna be okay like an innocent child, but at the same time would express her sassy attitude at the drop of a dime. Ashley had no problem putting Isis in her place or anyone on the set. It was kind of sexy how she did it in a nice-nasty kind of way. That was just a few things I liked and I was excited about getting to know her. The fact that she didn't have any baggage was a plus. No kids or baby daddy drama was a good thing.

Glad I caught her in the early stages of being a stripper. God only knows what she could've turned out to be. The only thing that did concern me however, was her relationship with Ray. He seemed to feel as though he owned her and a part of me felt like she was scared of him. No matter how she tried to hide behind those hazel eyes of hers, I could see the fear. I know I'd just met her and all, but I knew she was gonna be my new young tenderoni.

"I gotta leave and take care of some things, babe, see you in a couple of hours."

"Take me with you?" she begged in the most innocent tone she could muster.

"I can't. You know that."

"Pleaseeeeeeee."

She kissed me on the lips quickly.

"I can't, baby. But I'll meet you back at the house."

"Damn, alright. I'll be waiting," Ashley responded with a sexy pout, after seeing me walk away.

I blew her kisses all the way out of the door. Now, it was time to turn my phone back on and head to the office. After jumping in my Bentley, I immediately got into business mode. Dropping the top, I put my pedal to the metal and headed towards the freeway. My assistant, Charles, had left a message saying I needed to get to the office ASAP.

Hopefully he was bearing good news. Sometimes he could be so dramatic. Of course my wife made sure to hire a fucking homosexual as my assistant so there was no room for cheating. At the start of building my empire she was more involved. I was at the point in my life that I didn't want to feel the need for Charlotte's money. She tried her best to make me feel less of a man because she'd been so instrumental in my success. God willing, this reality show would take off and erase all my financial woes.

As soon as I walked in my office thirty minutes later, Charles bombarded me with drama. He was brightly dressed, as usual, with his Versace silk blouse and fuchsia, high-water skin-tight slacks.

"Top of the morning, Master Malcolm. Aren't you the topic on every gossip site including Wendy Williams?"

"What's new, Charles?"

"It's Charlize," he corrected me as if I would ever call him that shit. "Any who, I want to warn you that, a not so happy wife awaits in your office," he said, raising his eyebrows being extra animated.

"That's all I need, damn! How did she know that I was gonna be here today? You told her, didn't you?"

"Actually, she was notified by your lawyer, when he

called your home phone since you weren't answering your cell. The tabloids show you've been quite the busy guy.

"Don't cross the line, okay, Charles," I warned.

"Toodles," he said, raising his hand as he dismissed me.

Taking a deep breath, I walked in my office with no armor. I wasn't prepared for the next bout with my wife, but there was no avoiding her now. Even though there was a lot going on with the show and the media attention, I didn't have much time to devote to her drama.

"What the hell?" was the first thing that came to mind when I saw my wife's shaved head.

"That was rude. I really don't think you're in a place to criticize," Charlotte replied. She sat in my custom made leather executive chair that I'd ordered from Switzerland.

"Why the hell did you shave your head like that? What look are you going for Britney or Amber?"

"Okay, Diddy wanna-be. That's why you married me, because I look like Kim Porter. Guess I'm supposed to be her too, while you play with your side piece."

"Look, you're the one who wanted me to leave."

"Yeah, leave and take a small break, not fall in love with a fucking stripper."

I walked over to my small stainless steel refrigerator I kept in the corner and pulled out a bottle of Vitamin Water. "We're not together, she's my new project. I told you to stop listening to tabloids, Charlotte."

"Whatever, you liar. Who do you think is gonna believe that? Anyway, that's not why I'm here."

"That's surprising. Then why are you here?"

"I need you to come back home."

"Oh really?"

"My mom's cancer has come back and has taken a turn for the worse. The doctors let us know last week that she was in stage four of lymphoma and the cancer has now attacked her liver and kidneys. That's why I shaved my head. To help her deal with her new look since the chemo has made all her hair fall out again."

Within seconds, Charlotte let out a waterfall of tears as if she could no longer hold it together. I should've known that something bigger than my cheating was bothering her the way she was calm about the new drama reported about me. I felt bad for her. As close as Charlotte was with her mom I knew she needed me now more than ever.

She stood up. "You should know how it feels to watch your mom die. I need you, Malcolm, but if you're going to continue to bring stress into my life, then maybe it's best that we just legally separate."

I walked over to my wife, and gave her a comforting hug. "Sweetheart, I'll be there for you in any way you need me to."

She was right. To watch my mother die from AIDS was the hardest thing I'd ever experienced. My mother was a drug addict and her promiscuity landed her with the big disease with the little name. She was the reason why I sublimely hated drug dealers. It pained me to do business with them. They were maggots.

My wife knew that bringing my mother up would strike a chord and I found myself consoling her and sharing tears. She was in pain and I understood. As I held her close, she just went on and on about how she didn't understand why her mother was being punished when she was such a good woman.

"I need to get back to the hospital."

Charlotte quickly got herself together and put on her Tom Ford oversized shades to hide her tears. She then placed her head wrap on ready to exit. No matter what, she still was beautiful.

"Of course," I said, kissing her cheek. "Trust me, things will get better."

Just before Charlotte made it to the door, I got the shock of my life.

"Hello, Malcolm, remember me." A very heavy-set gentleman entered my office .He looked very familiar.

"Malcolm, I tried to tell him you were in a meeting and he still burst through the door. You want me to call the cops?" Charles followed behind scared to death.

"No, Charles, I can handle this," I assured.

"Is this your wife, Malcolm?" the guy asked.

"Yes, it is." I instantly gave him a look that said 'keep her out of this.'

"Oh, let me introduce myself. I'm Sharrod. One of your husband's business partners from Jersey."

"Hi Sharrod, I'm Charlotte. Malcolm, don't forget to pick up Gianni," Charlotte replied. "It was nice meeting you…"

"Sharrod."

Charlotte smiled. "Yes, Sharrod. Well, see you guys later."

Once Charlotte left the office, my heart pounded as lumps formed in my throat. It was him, the guy from the dinner with Sonny two years ago that helped dispose of Frankie and Pamela. I could never forget that scar. Now, I wondered if this was the last time I would ever see my wife. I immediately thought about my daughter and hoped to see her pretty little face again.

"How can I help you, Sharrod?" I sat down trying to keep my cool and not show my nervousness.

Sharrod took a seat in front of my desk. "I think you know why I'm here, it's time to pay up."

"Well, my family is going through a tough time right now. I let Sonny know that he would have his money by the end of the month."

"Yeah, he told me you would say that," Sharrod said, just before pulling out an oversized pocketknife. It was hard to keep my cool while he waved the neon blade around as he spoke.

"Man, come on. I'm a father. Don't do this. Do you have

kids? My daughter needs me." I pleaded.

"I'm a single father. But the difference between me and you is that I don't owe Sonny money, you do. Now, calm down, I'm not gonna kill you, yet. See, I'm here to collect some insurance for Sonny."

I slammed my hands on the desk frustrated. I could no longer compose myself.

"What does he want from me, what kind of…"

Before I could complete my sentence, Sharrod leaped across my desk and placed his big, fat fingers around my throat.

"Malcolm, give me a reason why I shouldn't kill you now. I hate it when somebody starts popping their gums at me. You think I'm a joke?"

"No, I don't Sharrod. I don't at all. Please don't kill me."

"Stop begging like a lil bitch, nigga!"

"Mannnnnnn, c'mon," I squealed.

After letting go, he pushed me across my desk. Papers flew everywhere. My heart thumped nonstop as sweat poured from my brow. I peeked at the picture of Gianni that had shattered on the floor.

"Sharrod, what can I do? What do you need from me?"

"This."

Just like that, Sharrod went straight for my hand. He caught my pinky right between his blade.

"Aighhhhhh shiiitttt!" I let out another huge squeal. No longer was my left pinky attached to my hand. The pain was so excruciating. Blood poured from my hand like a running faucet. The sight of all the blood made me instantly feel faint.

Picking up my pinky, Sharrod put it in his pocket as if it was business as usual. He ignored the blood gushing everywhere.

"This should hold Sonny's tiger Marty over for a minute. He's geeking for a treat."

"I need an ambulance!" I wailed.

"Now, if you didn't know before, you know now. Time

is money. Next time is gonna be that beautiful wife of yours."

"I'm gonna get him his money, damn! Leave my family out of this!" I yelled gasping for air.

"Then again, what's your new girl's name, Ashley, haha," Sharrod laughed as he left me in my office bleeding half to death.

I was losing so much blood by the second. Suddenly, I fell to the floor. Time was ticking and I needed Charlotte now more than ever.

Kennedi-14

"I need to make dinner reservations for Mr. and Mrs. Fitzgerald," I said jokingly, holding my new iPhone to my ear.

Standing over the loft in Malcom's penthouse I was quite pleased at how I was living now, and could definitely get used to this. It was a huge upgrade from living at Ray's raggedy ass apartment. Even better, it was an upgrade from my life as Kennedi. That girl was gone and I wasn't looking back. I had my eye on the prize. God had a plan for me and it was Malcolm. The reality show was highly anticipated and had landed me fame sooner than I could've imagined. Competing for a rappers love that I could care less about wasn't as hard as I thought. I mean, if I could fake like I enjoyed Sharrod's little dick, then I could do anything.

It was time for me to do my nightly ritual and take my bubble bath so when Malcolm got home I was ready to take care of him. He was gonna be my man if he knew it or not. Looking in the mirror, I looked at myself and envisioned my name being Ashley Fitzgerald. I also admired my new look. Even though I always had a decent length of hair, my new twenty-four inch extensions with highlights gave me a more Goddess look. Not to mention, the Botox Malcolm suggested I get along with fillers to accentuate my high cheek bones, really brought out my Asian features. It was crazy what money could do. Guess that's what came with being Malcolm's arm candy.

As I looked at myself naked, maybe Malcolm was right.

He wasn't a fan of all my piercings. The piercings I had below the belt definitely enhanced my orgasms, but the tongue piercing wasn't necessary, so I took it out.

Fantasizing a little more about my new life, I was interrupted by my cell phone. I left my phone in the kitchen, but it was only Malcolm calling. He was the only one with my new number. As I ran down the stairs, I slipped and fell over my shoe and missed his call. Before I could try and call him again he was sending me a text.

Babe, I'm not gonna make it home tonight. See you in a couple of days. Family emergency.

Oh, hell no. I was pissed off. What the hell was so important that he couldn't be here with me tonight? I called him immediately. As soon as he answered the phone, I went off.

"What do you mean you're not coming home? I cooked you dinner," I lied.

"Babe, my daughter's mother…"

"You mean your wife?"

"Look, my wife and I are not in a good place. Her mother is dying and she needs me."

Before he could go any further, I hung up on him. How did I become this girl? I was always the main chick and clowned bitches that weren't wifey. I was mad at myself for falling for him. Maybe I was coming across too thirsty that he'd lost respect for me. Maybe I was doing too much. Maybe I shouldn't have slept with him on the first night.

There were so many questions that ran across my mind and I needed answers. Even though Malcolm called back, I decided to not answer and sent him to voicemail. Fuck that bubble bath. He hated when I went out without him since the paparazzi always stalked us, but I was getting out of this damn penthouse to get some air. I didn't have anybody's phone numbers that I met because they were all in my old phone. The only person's number I knew by heart was Isis, so I decided to give her a call.

"Hello."

"What's up, Isis?"

"Who is this?"

"Ashley."

"What do you want?"

"I know you're not still mad about Malcolm."

"I don't get mad over dick, boo. He is one of many. Where are you calling me from?"

"This is my new phone number."

"I take it you still with him? I've been seeing you all on the blogs and shit lately," Isis said.

"You know I needed help and he was willing. You can't fault me for that."

"Fuck Malcolm! Furthermore, what the hell made you try to go off on Ray like that? He was pissed the fuck off. We ended up closing early that night."

"Fuck Ray, and I don't wanna talk about his ass either!" I spat. "You don't work tonight, do you?"

"No, but I'm on my way to pick up my money so I can go out tonight."

"Where are you going?" I inquired.

"Girl, me and Ginger are going to Greystone Manor. It's supposed to be popping tonight. One of the Lakers is hosting so we'll definitely be in the building."

"I wanna go. It's been a minute since I shook a tail feather."

"You want us to pick you up or you gonna meet us."

"I'll meet you there. What are you wearing?"

Isis laughed. "Something short and tight, of course."

"Cool. See you around midnight. I'll call you before I leave."

"Don't take forever. I'm not trying to be waiting all day for you at the door."

"I'll be ready."

"Okay, cool. See you in a little bit."

I didn't trust Isis one bit, but since I didn't have any girlfriends I had to bite the bullet in order to get out of the house. It was exciting that I was finally gonna get to explore L.A.'s club scene. I searched high and low for the keys to Malcolm's Maserati in the kitchen drawer. I was a superstar now and that meant no longer driving a damn Beetle. I had to look like money. My image was everything.

My life had changed so fast. Malcolm had filled one of the upstairs closets with many outfit choices, so I definitely had no problem finding something to wear. I decided on a red Herve Leger bandage dress with my new Louis Vuitton runway heels and handbag. I wet my hair a little more, added some mousse and was ready to go just in time.

It felt good to have a place to call home, that was nice, in the heart of downtown. But it would feel even better if Malcolm was with me. I tried to be positive and look at it on the bright side. At least he had blessed me this much so far. A part of me wished I hadn't called Isis and played my position. Maybe I shouldn't have reacted out of anger and hung up on him. Suppose he put me out. Then I thought it was best if I sent him a text and told him I understood so he didn't have second thoughts about me.

Baby, I'm sorry I hung up on you. Just had a romantic night planned. Take as much time as you need.

Cool, he responded, being real short.

Miss you.

He didn't respond.

Knowing he was probably pissed, instead of dwelling on it, I figured the best thing for me to do was enjoy my night. *$500 should be enough*, I thought to myself. Just before I walked out of the door, I was stopped in my tracks by an unexpected visitor. My heart felt like it had dropped to the pit of my stomach.

"Bad time, huh?"

"Oh my God, China, what the hell are you doing here? How did you get here?" I asked with a baffled look.

"Kasey brought me here. She said you had something to tell me."

"Where the fuck is Kasey?" I was furious.

My sister was apparently out for blood and wanted to destroy me. She'd made that perfectly clear with this stunt. So many emotions ran through me. China was the splitting image of Harry. Tears filled my eyes instantly. It felt as if all the breath had been taken from my body. I hadn't seen China since she was around three years old. I kept my distance because it was just too painful. If I had my choice I would've aborted her, but with the injuries of Tina beating me I was in the hospital my entire pregnancy. Big Mama promised to raise China as our sister if I didn't terminate the pregnancy. She talked me into giving her a chance at life. Seeing China now, made me relive my childhood, something that I kept buried deep inside.

"Hey sis," Kasey said, letting herself in with Chase in tow.

Surprisingly, she looked like money. Along with a huge diamond ring on her left hand, she also rocked designer shit from head to toe and carried a Rockstud Valentino bag. I couldn't believe it. She actually looked more like me than ever. I also couldn't help staring at her massive ring. Questions filled my head. Was she engaged? Who could've given her ass a ring that size?

"Kennedi! You look so pretty. I love you so much, Kennedi! I missed you. Auntie said this is our new house!" Chase yelled all excited grabbing me around the waist. He'd gotten so big in the two years I'd been gone.

My eyes widened with shock. I couldn't believe that Chase had just called me by my first name. "Chase, you're not allowed to call me that."

He looked back and forth between me and my sister. "But Auntie said that you didn't deserve to be called Mommy anymore and that I would get in trouble if I said it."

It was a stabbing betrayal on Kasey's part. But then

again, what did I care? I didn't want to be anybody's mother anymore, so it really didn't matter. Besides, I had more important things to address.

"Kasey, how did you know where to find me? How did you get upstairs? Why did you bring them here?" I whispered as if Malcolm was in the next room. I needed to be more aware of my surroundings if she could find me so easily.

Making her way inside, Kasey took off her five inch YSL pumps like she was at home, which pissed me off.

"Well, that's not hard to figure out. Don't you realize how much you and your new man stay in the media? Besides, we're twins, remember, so the doormen downstairs thought I was you. And by the way, I hate the new name you chose. Ashley Jacobs...really? Sounds like a white girl," Kasey informed. "Plus, since you're rich now, I thought it was best to bring your kids to you. No need for me to be taking care of them anymore."

"What do you mean kids?" China asked. "You not leaving me with her."

Her demeanor was too much. She bobbed her head with attitude as her hands graced her little ten year-old hips.

"China, that's why we're here. Now that you're getting older, it's time you knew the truth. Mona isn't your mother, Kennedi is," Kasey informed.

"Huh?" China cut her eyes at me with a confused expression.

"Stop lying to her, Kasey. Get the fuck out of my house! You lying bitch! All I ever did, all my life was protect you. Just when you see my life going well you try to sabotage me!" I screamed.

"What have you ever done for me, Kennedi? Nothing. Get over yourself and stop faking like I made you so fucked up," Kasey countered.

"Auntie, Kennedi, stop fighting all the time," Chase interrupted. Ignoring him we continued to fuss.

I pointed towards the door. "Get out before I call security! I have somewhere to be!"

"It's true, ain't it? That's why you all mad. Why y'all lie to me," China's grown ass said, getting all up in my face.

"No, China. I'm your sister. I'm not your mother. Kasey is just trying to bring me down," I lied looking her dead in her hazel eyes that were identical to mine. That hurt.

"Kennedi, can I stay here with you? Can I play with her?" Chase pointed to the picture of Gianni.

"So, you playing house with this nigga's daughter, but cant take care of your own? I don't know why I ever subjected these kids by bringing them here. Come on y'all, let's go," Kasey said.

"Yeah, get the fuck out!" I shot back.

"Kennedi, I wanna stay with you. Why do we have to leave, we just got here," Chase whined.

"You can't stay with me right now, Chase. Just give me some time. I'll come back for you," I lied again. Anything to get them the fuck out of my house.

Kasey rolled her eyes. "Don't sell him no dreams, bitch. He's good. We'll make sure of that. I see this fame hasn't changed you. Still the same selfish bitch you always were."

"Kasey, don't ever show your face here again!" I said, slamming the door. Now more than ever I needed a drink.

Kennedi-15

Finally, a night out, it was definitely needed after what I'd just gone through. It was a must that I had a good time. As soon as I pulled up in front of the club in Malcolm's Maserati, all eyes were on me. As soon as Ginger spotted me, she ran up and gave me a hug. I hadn't seen her since I left the Playas Mansion.

"Hey, sexy girl."

"Hey, Ginger, how the hell are you?"

"I'm good. You ready to have a ball or two or four."

I giggled. "Girl, you're crazy."

"Hey, Ice, Ice baby," I greeted.

"What's up, phat ta death? Did Malcolm let you drive that bad ass car?" Isis asked hating.

"Y'all ready to show me a fun night in L.A.?" I asked, ignoring her comment.

"Hell yeah," Ginger replied excited as hell. "Girl, you gotta tell me, how the hell you landed Malcolm Fitzgerald and all this fame that quick."

"She got good pussy, that's how. It's nice and wet," Isis chimed in.

"Hey, ladies I don't really wanna talk about me tonight, I just wanna have fun," I replied with a 'can we drop this shit' tone.

As we walked up to the door the line was ridiculous. Trying to see just how much pull Isis had, I fell a few steps behind, acting as if I was fixing my shoe. Just as I suspected, the bouncer turned her ass away just like the peon I knew she was.

Me however…I just walked up to the rope with Ginger's arm wrapped around mine and they immediately opened the rope and nodded. After getting our VIP bands, I finally gave the okay that Isis was with us. As annoyed as I was with her, I wanted to show her who was boss.

"Just like I thought, no pull." I giggled to Ginger. "How the fuck is this your city and you can't get in the club?" I continued to instigate.

"That's a new bouncer and I haven't been out in a long time," Isis faked.

"But I'm not even from here and they let us right in with no problem," I countered.

"You're a stripper, Ashley. You're gonna always be able to get in a club with no problem," Isis shot back.

"No, I think it's my new life with Malcolm. I'm not a dancer anymore, sweetheart," I said unbothered.

"Hey, let's party!" Ginger barged into the conversation.

"I couldn't agree more!" I yelled as I sang along to the song, *Paparazzi. Paparazzi on my back, paparazzi on my back, strike a pose, strike a pose, strike a pose, you snatched!*

After getting a table, we ordered bottles of Moet and Ciroc. Ginger downed her peach Ciroc and I shot back Patron shots and Moet all night. Isis, on the other hand, was stand-offish and really wasn't with us the majority of the night. She hooked up with some of the other girls that danced at Playas Mansion which was fine by me.

Ginger and I had a blast. After all the drama I faced before coming out, this was well needed. By the time the club was minutes away from closing and we paid our bill, I was drunk as shit. It was time to call it a night.

"Where the hell is my car? I paid you extra to keep my shit parked out front," I snapped at the valet guy. It was annoying to have to wait when I should've been considered VIP. "This type of shit is unacceptable!" All of a sudden, flashing cameras bombarded me.

"Ashley, how long have you've been seeing Malcolm Fitzgerald?" someone yelled.

"How's the show coming along?" another person yelled.

"Are you seeing Malcom and Neko Luv at the same time?" a third person belted.

Any question you could imagine came at me. While I tried to shield my face, Ginger loved the attention.

I couldn't have been happier when the valet guy finally appeared, but it quickly dawned on me that he came back without the car.

"What happened? What's taking so long?" I asked.

"Ma'am, someone flattened all of the tires on your vehicle," he informed me. "All four of them are ruined."

"What? Are you serious?" *What the hell am I going to tell Malcolm*, was all I could think of? Who would do such a thing?

Conveniently, Isis pulled up moments later. "Y'all good."

"No, somebody flattened my damn tires. I was gonna take Ginger home since you were about to leave her. We both need a ride."

"Damn, haters never sleep." Isis smirked. "Are you gonna wait for a tow truck, Ashley?"

I shook my head. "No, I'll do that shit later. Too many paparazzi out here." They continued to take pictures and call out my name.

"Come on y'all. Ginger, I'll drop you off first," Isis responded.

"Cool beans," Ginger said as she jumped in the front seat.

Drunk out of my mind, I was tired and so out of it I decided to take a quick nap until we got to the penthouse. However, when I finally woke up I was confused as hell about where I was. I was cold and completely naked. It was dark and the room reeked of cigarette and weed smoke.

"Rise and shine tough guy," I heard a man say.

My eyes enlarged as I quickly sat up. Hearing that familiar voice, I knew exactly where I was. I also knew that bitch Isis had set me up.

Ray lit up a cigarette. "Ya' ready ta give up dat pussy now?" he asked just before placing the cigarette near my bare stomach.

"Leave me the hell alone. Don't come near me!" I yelled.

"Why ya don't wanna give me da pussy anymore. Is it because ya tink ya some kind of hot shot now? Ya tink ya a big star? Since boss-lady said I can't kill ya, I'm only left with one ting."

"What are you talking about?"

"I told Shawn about ya flippin' out and told her I was gonna slit ya throat. She said I couldn't, but didn't say nuthin' about me takin' da punani."

"Please don't, Ray," I pleaded.

He pulled out a gun as I jumped up and attempted to run. I didn't get far before he grabbed me by my hair and yanked my body back towards him. I desperately wanted to wake up from this nightmare.

Escaping his grasp for a second, Ray caught me again when I tripped over a pile of clothes. At that moment, he pushed me onto the floor and climbed on top of me. Why me? Why did I have to go through this shit again? I prayed to God to save me from this hell. Then again, maybe I was being punished for dismissing my kids.

"I thought ya wanted dis," Ray whispered right before punching me in my face. "Open ya legs!"

"No, Ray please you can't. I have AIDS," I thought of anything to get him to stop.

"Well, so do I," he said, sucking my neck.

His disgusting moaning gave me instant flashbacks of my childhood. Now, here I was reliving that moment as Ray started to stuff his dick inside of me. There was no way I could get away with his gun to my head.

"Ya finally got this dick, how it feel to ya? Big ain't it."

"Stop please," I cried as he pumped harder and harder. His grunting made me sick. I felt dizzy.

"Ya pussy is so good. Damn, I should've fucked ya a long time ago."

The pain of Ray ramming his dick inside of me made me nauseous so I started throwing up. But he didn't care. His nasty ass just continued to thrust himself in and out.

"Ahh shit, ahh damn, ahh," Ray moaned as he ejaculated inside of me moments later.

"Oh my, God. You came in me?"

"Ya on da pill, right?"

"No, I'm not asshole!" I yelled then covered up. "I hope you fucking burn in hell for doing this to me."

Ray flaunted a devious smirk. "Get ya shit out my place and never cross my path again, or next time I won't be dat generous to spare ya life."

"You will pay!" I threatened while looking for my clothes. My body was in pain and I reeked of vomit.

"I know ya bizness, Ashley, so I advise ya not to try me. I'm sure ya don't want ya secret life exposed. I don't think Malcolm will like it."

I couldn't help but wonder what he meant by knowing my business. My heart sunk in my stomach. As I gathered my things and threw them in a trash bag, I wondered how I was gonna get back to the penthouse at five a.m.

"Every little ting, is gonna be alright."

As I listened to Ray sing a Bob Marley tune in the shower the angrier I got. He'd just raped me and obviously felt that it was okay to sing to the top of his lungs like everything was all good. There was no way I was going out like a sucker with that bastard having my life story over my head. I was pissed that Shawn had told him my business, and even worse betrayed me like this.

After I got all my belongings and the money I'd stashed in the apartment, I put everything by the door. The closer I got to the bathroom the more nervous I became, but I knew what I had to do. I'd made a promise to myself a long time ago, there was no way a man would violate me again and get away with it.

The more Ray sung as if he'd just hit the lottery, the angrier I became. As I peeked in the door, I could see the gun sitting on the back of the toilet. I took a deep breath knowing this was the right thing to do. When Ray was just about to turn the water off, I immediately took off running going for the gun.

"Shut the fuck up, you bastard!" I screamed as soon as the firearm was safely in my hands.

"Bumbaclot bitch. If ya got da balls to point a gun at me and tink ya gonna get away with it, then pull da trigga!" Ray yelled.

I did just that. After one shot to the head, his body collapsed to the floor. Making sure he was gone, I walked over and placed the gun to his temple, and fired another round. Blood gushed everywhere. I guess being involved with Sharrod had allowed me to kill a little easier than I thought.

"Oh my God Ashley, what have you done? Ray! Ray!"

Isis stood in the doorway with a pair of handcuffs in her hand along with a black bag. It was clear who the handcuffs were for, but I could only imagine what her sick ass had in the bag.

"It looks like you were about to have some fun, but you missed the party, bitch," I said.

She never took her eyes off Ray's body. "Ray!"

"Bitch, you set me up."

Isis had tears in her eyes. "I'm calling the cops."

"Oh no you're not!"

Before she could even think about pulling her phone out, I directed the gun toward her chest. She let out a terrifying scream right before collapsing onto the dark hardwood floor.

I'd obviously sent her straight to hell right along with her fucking boss.

After cleaning up every bit of my DNA out of that apartment, I grabbed Ray's .32 for protection and finally kissed that hell hole goodbye. As I walked down the street in search for a cab, I was scared as hell. It felt like the streets were watching. What had I done? Just like that my life had changed. Killing two people was never in my plans. What was I thinking? Supposed someone came after me. I felt nervous and alone.

There wasn't a cab in site and it seemed as if I'd been walking forever. After walking about ten more blocks with that heavy ass trash bag, finally I got a cab. I was ready to just get home, get in the shower, and wash that nasty Jamaican bastard off of me.

When the driver finally pulled up to the building, I quickly paid the fare and jumped out, thankful that there were no photographers in sight. The tears that I held back for so long finally came out as I walked inside the house. All I wanted to do was sleep this nightmare away. Getting in the shower and letting the water run all over me was a step closer to making me feel a little better. Once I got out, I lit the fireplace and burned the clothes I had on and hid the gun. Knowing I would need some help getting to sleep, I popped an Ambien then slowly made my way back to the bedroom wishing Malcolm was here to console me.

I was awakened by a slow kiss all over my neck, which instantly freaked me out.

"Get the fuck off me!" I yelled, then jumped up.

"Baby, it's me, what's wrong? What the hell happened to you?" Malcolm asked with concern after seeing my face.

"Oh my goodness Malcolm, what happened to you?" His face was badly beaten as well and his entire hand was bandaged. We both looked like shit.

"Baby, I'm sorry. Oh my God they got to you, too. I'm so sorry, Ashley. I should've never left you here alone."

"Who got to me?"

"Ahhhhhhh, shit!"

Malcolm just covered his face with his palms. He was scaring the shit outta me.

"Just hold me," I said confused at what the hell he was talking about.

"Baby, I'm right here. Everything is gonna be okay."

"What happened to your hand, Malcolm? Your finger, oh my God."

"It's nothing that plastic surgery can't fix. Don't worry baby everything is gonna be fine. I'm sorry for putting you in the middle of my shit."

What the hell was Malcolm caught up in that he thought someone had attacked me, too? It was a good thing that I'd decided to keep Ray's gun. The smart thing was to go along with whatever he thought happened. No one could know I killed Ray. Not even Malcolm.

Malcolm-16

"Hello."

"Malcolm, it's Sonny. How's the hand? Marty really appreciated the treat."

"Sonny, I'm gonna send the wire transfer by the end of the day. I promise."

My anxiety level had increased drastically, just that fast.

"Malcolm, I didn't call for a bunch of excuses. You and that maggot nephew of mine have been a liability since this shit started. I invested in the project expecting revenue and all we've gotten is a bunch of niggas fighting every night. This was supposed to be a classy spot and it's everything but that. Rappers hang out there, Malcolm! That wasn't the vision we discussed and the money isn't there. I've lost way too much money and I want all that I invested in this bullshit project no later than five p.m."

"Five p.m. sounds fine."

"I don't want to make an example out of you, Malcolm. I think you're a great guy, and that wife of yours, Charlotte, she's a doll. I never understood why you started banging that stripper chick. Your wife has so much class."

He knew way too much, which made this situation even worse.

"Furthermore, you need to be around to raise Gianni. I saw your nanny taking her to school the other day. Beautiful little girl," Sonny continued with his rant.

"Sonny, you'll get your money. Keep my family out of this."

"Today, five p.m., no later."

Click.

Now that my family was being threatened, Charlotte had to get me that money fast or all of our lives were on the line. I knew she was going to be mad at me for not coming home last night, but I couldn't leave Ashley. She seemed a bit off lately and I didn't want to lose her. Falling for her was never my intentions. It was just something about Ashley that I needed in my life right now.

It was tough to constantly be torn between my family and my new guilty pleasure. I was used to having my cake and eating it too, but something made me only want Ashley. If I could still have the money from Charlotte and my daughter, that would be ideal.

Here goes nothing, I whispered to myself as I hit speed dial and phoned my wife. When she answered the phone pissed off, I knew I had a lot of work to do in order to get the money.

"What do you want, Malcolm?"

"We need to talk."

"Talk about what? What makes you think that you can just come and go as you please. Who the hell do you think you are? My mom is fighting for her life and here I am dealing with your bullshit!" she spat.

"Look, I know you're mad, but it is imperative that you help me."

"Ask that bimbo you're sleeping with to help you. Oh, that's right, you can't. I guess she didn't make enough tips on the pole to afford your financial woes. Do you think I'm going to support you and your side hoe? You must be tripping?"

"Charlotte, our lives are in jeopardy. I have until five p.m. to pay a ten million dollar debt."

"Not my problem." She seemed completely unfazed.

"They know where Gianni goes to school!"

"That's public knowledge. Hell, even the paparazzi knows that. You're gonna have to come up with something better," Charlotte said with a slight chuckle.

"Do you value your life? These people aren't playing. Do you think my finger just fell off my hand?"

"First, you told me it was a freak accident on the set. Now, someone cut your finger off. Do I look that stupid to you?"

"Charlotte, if you're upset about who I fuck from time to time because my wife never wants to give up the pussy, then that's fine. But when it comes to my daughter's life being in jeopardy, that's when all that other shit needs to be put to the side." I'm sure Charlotte probably turned a shade darker by my last comment.

"How dare you? The reason why we're not having sex is because of your lack of respect for this marriage. Maybe I will start fucking one of the many A-list actors who question me on a regular about why I stay with your ass. Then you'll see how it feels. Yeah, maybe that's what I'll do."

"Well, go do it then!" I was sick of her threats, and now wasn't a good time.

Click.

Hanging up on her ass was the easy way out. It was the only way I could control how angry I was. By me having my money tied up in so many things it would be difficult to get my hands on ten million dollars by five p.m. If I'd been a single man, I probably would've just taken my chances and left the country for a while. Maybe even get a few international deals going on. But by me having a family, I had to figure out a way to make this shit work. I felt bad for putting their lives in jeopardy. Needing to go somewhere and think, I put the pedal to the metal and drove straight to my penthouse.

As soon as I pulled into my garage I had a strange feeling that I was being watched. I was used to the paparazzi stalking a nigga, but this felt different. After quickly making my way to the top floor and placing my key inside the door, I was surprised to see Ashley sitting on the couch Indian style crying like a baby.

"Babe, what's wrong?" I asked shutting the door.

"Nothing. I just miss you. I don't know if I can do this. I'm falling for you, and I deserve you to myself," she cried.

"No, really what's wrong? I've never seen you like this."

"I don't know. I've been very emotional lately. My allergies have been bothering me, and I feel like a mess," she replied.

"I'm going through a lot right now, and I came here to think. I was hoping that you could make me feel better. You make me smile and I need that right now." I caressed her arm. "But seeing you this upset, it looks like I need to figure out what's wrong with you first, so, let's talk."

"I guess that's why I fell for you." She hit me with a seductive smile. "Even when you're going through something you're still thinking of me."

"Why wouldn't I?"

"Let's be real. Most men think of themselves first."

"Nah, not me. When you need me, I'm there."

Before I could continue, Ashley was on top of me with her tongue down my throat. She was so forceful.

"Make love to me, Malcolm. Make me feel better."

She didn't have to tell me that twice. Removing the t-shirt from her perfect hourglass figure, I licked my lips after looking at her pierced nipples. For the moment, all my problems disappeared.

"I can't wait to taste you," I stated.

"This is your temple. Do as you please." Ashley smiled exposing her left dimple. All she had to do was smile for me and everything just felt better.

My dick was harder than a week old bagel as I carried her up the stairs to the bedroom. As soon as I placed her on the bed, once again I looked at her perfect body which instantly reminded me of the first time I met her in Playas Mansion. Who would've thought that I would fall for one of Ray's girls, after going there all these years? Hell, I'd fucked plenty of strippers in the past, but never thought I'd catch feelings for one. I had to admit…it felt good that she belonged to me now.

As if Ashley read my mind, she rolled over onto her stomach and spread her legs wide open. Of course, I couldn't help spanking her ass, and even smiled when it jiggled. I couldn't take it anymore. Diving into her nest, I made love to her with my tongue. Her shaven vagina was so perfect.

"Ahh, Malcolm you make me feel so good, baby. I love you," Ashley moaned.

"Malcolm Fitzgerald, I can't believe you!"

I knew that voice from anywhere. It was Charlotte. In all the years we'd been married, she'd never popped up at my penthouse. Why now? By her catching me sucking Ashley's pussy, there was no way in hell I was getting out of this one. Finally, I'd been caught.

I turned around so fast I almost got whiplash, "What are you doing here?"

"What the fuck do you mean, what am I doing here? You bastard!" Charlotte instantly charged at me like a bull.

"Stop it, Charlotte!" I yelled while dodging her wild swings.

"Fuck you! I can't believe you keep doing this to me. I'm your wife!" Charlotte swung at me a few more times before directing her attention to Ashley. "Do you know he's married?"

Ashley didn't seem phased at all by Charlotte's presence. "Sweetheart, I don't care if he's married or not. And furthermore I don't owe you anything. Now, if you would excuse us, we were in the middle of something. Like you kinda fucked up my orgasm."

"You bitch!" Charlotte roared before smacking the shit out of Ashley.

Before I could get in between them, Ashley started wailing on my wife. Charlotte was never a fighter. She was always violent towards me, but never another woman.

"Stop it!" I yelled before Ashley let out an ear piercing scream.

"My nipple ring!"

"You whore!" Charlotte yelled as blood gushed out of Ashley's left breast. "If this is the type of image you were going for? Why did you marry me, Malcolm?" my wife asked with tears in her eyes.

"This is not the time for this Charlotte, can't you see she's bleeding." I pointed to Ashley.

"Are you serious, Malcolm?" By this time, tears streamed down Charlotte's face. "Do you love her?"

"Ahhh, Malcolm it hurts so bad," Ashley cried as I carried her to the bathroom.

"Here let me get some alcohol." There was no way I was gonna answer Charlotte's question.

"You know what Malcolm, I'm done with you. You call me begging for money, and when I tell you no, the first thing you do is come here and fuck this bitch. If this is the type of chick you want on your arm you can have her!"

Charlotte rambled on and on. I ignored her as I tried to stop Ashley from bleeding. As she yelled out obscenities, the last comment she made got the attention of both me and Ashley.

"Guess you haven't seen the latest cover of *In Touch Weekly*. How embarrassing? Out of all the whores you've cheated with, this one is the worst. I guess you dug deep in the gutter for this one. I bet you don't even know her real name," Charlotte said.

Ashley immediately jumped up and went into attack mode. They started fighting again. That poor wounded Ashley was no longer in sight. She went after Charlotte as if she had something to hide. After several attempts, I broke them up from fighting again by getting in between them. This time I held onto Ashley.

"Bitch, I'm tired of your mouth, you don't know me!" Ashley screamed.

"Ashley? Oh that's what your name is supposed to be?" Charlotte questioned with a smirk.

"My name is Ashley!"

Charlotte shook her head. "Well, this magazine doesn't say that. My daughter and I were in the grocery store today shopping and she pulled this off of the shelf because she saw her father's face on the cover."

"Charlotte, those dumb magazines are always making up shit. You know that," I butted in.

"So, I guess they photoshopped a mug shot of your girlfriend, too, huh?" Charlotte smiled even harder this time. "You're sitting here eating out a convicted felon dumb ass."

When Charlotte threw the *Hip Hop Star* magazine on the floor, both me and Ashley's eyes lit up like fireworks. There it was, her mug shot along with a caption that read, *Malcolm's Mistress is a Convicted Felon.*

"Her ass failed to tell you that she ran a drug cartel in New Jersey, Malcolm," Charlotte said.

Before I could even respond there was a loud knock on the door.

"So, who the fuck is that, Malcolm, another trick? Were you all planning to have some type of threesome," Charlotte badgered.

"Hell no. I don't know who that is," I replied as the knocks continued.

"Mr. Fitzgerald, it's the police!" I suddenly heard a man yell.

My neighbors must've heard the ruckus in my house and called the cops. *I can't believe I came here to think about my situation with Sonny and now I'm going through this shit*, I thought. I knew the police weren't gonna go away, so I decided to make my way downstairs. The sooner I got rid of them, the sooner I could get rid of Charlotte.

Charlotte was right on my heels, when I opened the door.

"Umm, Mr. Fitzgerald, we've gotten several calls about screaming coming from your unit. Is everything alright in here?" the shorter white officer questioned.

"No, it's not. I just caught my husband sucking a criminal's pussy!" Charlotte ranted.

As the officer turned beet red, Ashley walked downstairs with one of my t-shirts on.

"Ma'am, you're bleeding. Is everything okay?" the black officer asked, then walked over to her.

"I'm fine, but can you guys just please remove that crazy woman from my home?" Ashley asked politely.

Charlotte looked possessed when she turned to Ashley. "Your home? Bitch, are you delusional? This is *my* shit! I make everything possible for Malcolm. His ass is broke! *My* money keeps your ass in Gucci and gold, not his!"

"So, Mr. Fitzgerald, what would you like us to do? This issue has to be resolved so your neighbors don't have a reason to call us back," the white officer stated.

I looked at both Ashley and Charlotte for a few seconds. One of them had to go. "Yes, officers can you please remove this crazy woman from our home," I said, pointing to Charlotte.

"Ma'am, please come with us," the white officer said, as he gently placed his hands around Charlotte's arm to escort her out.

Even though I deserved all the names my wife called me on her way out of the door, it was best that she left so I could get some answers from Ashley. After looking at the magazine, I needed to know who I'd fallen in love with. What was Ashley hiding?

Kennedi–17

"It looks like you have some explaining to do," Malcolm said with a look of hurt and disappointment.

What the hell just happened, I thought to myself.

All the hard work I'd put into keeping my secret hidden from Malcolm, to get exposed by his wife was never a thought. I didn't know what to say and I was at a loss for words. I needed to know exactly what the magazine said. I was nervous as hell. All my life I dreamed of landing a man like Malcolm and to come this close and lose everything wasn't an option.

"Look, Malcolm, I'm not a bad person."

"Who are you? Is your name even, Ashley?"

Before I could answer, Malcolm's phone rang. The more he pressed ignore, the more they kept calling back.

"What's up?" he answered, annoyed as hell. After listening briefly, Malcolm excused himself from the room. Any other time Malcolm would take calls in front of me, why not now? *Was that a bitch,* I wondered. I wasn't about to let another chick take my spot. Not even his bitch ass wife.

My mind did backflips as I tried to think fast. How was I gonna get out of this one? Since it appeared as if Malcolm was gonna be on the phone for a while, I decided to go upstairs and get myself together. I figured maybe if we went out to a romantic dinner, we could talk. That would at least buy me some time. Right as I was getting out of the shower, I heard Malcolm's footsteps as they walked into the room. My heart throbbed. I still didn't know what to say.

"I need some answers. Who are you?" he questioned me with a puzzled look.

"There is a lot about me you need to know, but I'd prefer to talk over dinner," I said casually, while drying off.

"We're not going anywhere until you explain this damn mug shot!" Malcolm had never raised his voice at me. He was so on edge.

"So, you tell me not to pay attention to the tabloids, but here you are feeding into them. Maybe this shit we have ain't real after all. After opening my heart to you this is how I get treated? Your wife comes in here and attacks me and I get ridiculed."

"I saved your life, Ashley! Rescuing you from the strip club wasn't enough? Look, I don't have time or patience for games. I have too much other shit to worry about and I can't have a fraud in my life. Let's cut to the chase. What's your deal? Who are you? Explain this article."

This was the first time I'd ever seen him this upset. There was no way I was dodging this situation. Picking up the magazine, I went straight to the article that had a picture of me as big as day. *If I would've agreed to the witness protection program this wouldn't be happening*, I thought to myself. As I skimmed the page before I spoke, a story started to spill out. Before I could catch myself, I was lying again.

"Malcolm, my real name is Ashley, but I have a twin sister named Kennedi. This is who this article is about, not me. Yes, I've shoplifted before when I was younger because we were in foster care, but I'm not a bad person. That's the only thing I've ever done wrong. I promise. You have to believe me. I love you. I would never lie to you," I pleaded as tears flowed from my eyes.

"You have a sister, a twin?"

"Yes. She's a real piece of work, and part of the reason why I left home and moved away. I needed to escape all the negativity. When I thought life could be better, it got harder. That's when I met Ray and started dancing. I'm so embarrassed," I cried out. As snot dripped from my nose, Malcolm came closer to me. His posture turned from disappointment to concern.

"Sweetheart, I love you, but you have to be honest with me. There's so much shit going on in my life right now and I need people around me who are genuine."

"I am Malcolm, I am. I need you to believe me!" I continued to cry real tears. I was on an emotional rollercoaster. Malcolm was all I had and I couldn't lose him now.

"Promise me that you'll always be honest with me."

I shook my head. "I promise, Malcolm. You're the best thing that has ever happened to me. I need you in my life."

"The first night I met you, I told you that I would take care of you. All I want in return is honesty. There's nothing that you can't tell me. You got me. I got you," he said, looking deep in my tear filled eyes.

Malcolm reached out and held me tight in his strong build. From the way he held me, I could tell that he really did have something else going on besides wifey drama.

"I think we both need a breather. How about that dinner?"

"Damn right. Let's get the hell out of here."

That was a close call, I thought to myself as I climbed in the Bentley's front seat. For the first time, I felt like Malcolm's girl. For so long I felt like his jump off, but today he made me feel special the way he defended me to his lame ass wife. I was in it for keeps and there was nothing that was going to tear us apart, not even Charlotte. I couldn't believe how desperate she sounded lying about how Malcolm was broke. That chick was a character.

"Shit, it's after five," Malcolm mumbled as his phone slipped between the seats.

"Am I ruining your evening plans, did you have somewhere to be?" I questioned.

"No, just had a deadline, that's all. Nothing I can really do about it," he said, brushing it off.

Reaching between the seats, I grabbed his phone and handed it to him. The way his phone kept ringing it was hard to believe that he was telling me the truth, something was up. I was getting annoyed by the second. I wanted to ask him so bad who the hell was calling, and why he wasn't answering. But now wasn't the time to be a nag. Malcolm's deep sigh as he pressed ignore on his cell, showed that whoever it was, he didn't want to talk to. All I knew was that Miss Ashley Jacobs was in the passenger seat of this Bentley to stay. There was no way I was losing my position.

"So, babe, have you heard anything from Ray since you left the club? I've been hearing all types of crazy shit like that nigga hasn't been home or to the club in a minute. People are saying he's missing. That club is his life, so something must've gone down."

Lumps formed in my throat; he caught me off guard.

"No, and I don't give a fuck where he is. Maybe he's in Jamaica or something, but who really cares," I snapped, "You haven't talked to your girl, Isis," I shot back knowing that would get him to change the subject quick.

"Naw, no need. I got you," Malcolm smiled as he leaned back and got in cruise mode.

As the old school song, *Forever My Lady* by Jodeci blared through the speakers my mind wondered off to life with Sharrod. Malcolm was in another league that Sharrod could never imagine. Having Malcolm in my life was a blessing, but it was hard to take it all in knowing I was living a lie. Me killing Ray and Isis constantly kept my mind unsettled. Kasey knowing where I stayed was another weight on my back. With all the skeletons I had, I wished so bad I could just tell Malcolm the truth about everything, but my gut just wouldn't allow me to.

"What are you over there in deep thought about?"

"You. Malcolm, I meant it when I told you I loved you, so I want you to be honest with me about something. Why have you been so jumpy lately? What really happened to your hand?"

"Nothing you have to worry your pretty heart about."

"Tell me something, you cut it slicing your steak, anything. I'm a ride or die chick. You can tell me if somebody been bothering my baby," I joked.

"I'm fine, Ashley, okay?" Malcolm snapped.

"Sorry," I said, lowering my head as if my feelings were hurt.

"No, I'm sorry. We're gonna be good. I just don't want my lady worrying about nothing," Malcolm replied, putting his hand in mine as we made a right turn onto North Canon Drive. "Hope you have an appetite."

"I'm starving. Where are we going?"

"Mastro's. Ever been?"

"No, but I'm sure it's great."

Once we pulled up to the valet, the paparazzi were on the prowl. Snapping photos and blurting out numerous questions that ticked me off about my past life was annoying. I always wanted the fame, but being exposed wasn't fun. Suddenly, we were ushered through the crowd by one of Malcolm's security guards, Jason. Where he came from I had no clue, but I was glad to see him.

"Does the increase in security have anything to do with your hand?" I pried.

"Give it up, Ashley. Let's just enjoy our night," Malcolm whispered under his breath as we finally made it into the restaurant.

Once we approached the hostess station, I was mesmerized by the restaurant's décor. The beautiful red light fixture was gorgeous. All this time I thought Ruth Chris was for the rich, but Mastro's was in another league. I would've never been able to experience this life without Malcolm. The restaurant was packed and there was a two-hour wait, but of course with Malcolm's status we were seated immediately.

"Mr. Fitzgerald, welcome back. Are you going to order outside of your usual?" the busty white waitress questioned with a smile.

"I'll have my usual; Ash, do you know what you want yet?" Malcolm questioned.

"What's good here?"

"Everything. You can't go wrong."

"Okay, then I'll start with the warm spinach salad. The Chilean sea bass sounds great, too, with the lobster mac-n-cheese."

Before I could complete my order, we were suddenly bombarded by a white Italian chick that I'd seen on many videos. She even made it through the three big security guys who guarded us.

"Malcolm, I will not be fucking ignored!" she demanded.

He looked as if he'd seen a ghost. "Cherry, what are you doing here?"

"So, I have to hunt you down to talk to you now? Do you want me to go to the magazines to get through to you or are you gonna listen?" Cherry spat.

"Sweetheart, we've had a long night and me nor Malcolm have the energy for anymore drama. If he used to fuck you and you're having trouble with rejection, then deal with it. We're together now," I informed her.

"Look little wanna-be, I don't take advice from the next bitch. Let Malcolm tell me he's done," Cherry countered.

We both looked at Malcolm for a response.

"Cherry, we're done," he finally spoke.

"Thank you. Now, remove yourself from our table before I have my security remove you." I hoped to humiliate her as much as possible.

"Jason would never remove me from this table. We go way back. As for you, Malcolm, I'll just see you in court!" Cherry yelled.

Malcolm frowned. "Court for what. We don't have any business dealings together."

"Oh, yes we do, your one-year old son, Malcolm Jr., who I call MJ. So, here you go, court papers for child support and your last name."

Malcolm didn't even bother to look at the paperwork. "Cherry, you are crazy? We never fucked without a condom, and furthermore you don't even have any kids."

"That's where you're wrong, Malcolm. Remember the first night we met, when I insisted on using my own condom? How lucky was I that I was ovulating?" Cherry let out a wicked little laugh.

"Jason, I need her gone. I don't have time for this shit." Malcolm motioned for his security.

"I'm leaving, but before I go take a look at this picture and tell me you can deny him," Cherry added.

As she slapped the picture of her son on the table, Malcolm sat paralyzed. I tried to sneak a peak at the picture before Malcolm swiped it to the floor. My heart dropped. I wasn't sure if I could deal with two rug rats.

"Why now, Cherry? Why now? With all I've done for your career. Where is he?" Malcolm asked.

"He's in Atlantic City with my mom."

"But, why now? I need a fucking blood test."

"Why now, Malcolm? I'll tell you why. Because I'm tired of being a throw away doll when you find a new chick. He'll do you the same way." Cherry warned me as I shrugged my shoulders.

Malcolm threw up his hands. "But why didn't you tell me, Cherry? How do I know he's mine?"

"Because it's your turn to care for him. My mom is asking for more money. I have a career now and it's too much to deal with. I just can't," Cherry said just before running out of the restaurant.

At the moment, she reminded me of myself in a way. Malcolm's drama was a little more than I was prepared for. I was definitely getting on my knees tonight to pray that little boy wasn't his.

Malcolm-18

As I peered at my cell phone while we exited the church, the text message from an unknown number appeared on my phone

Malcolm, your time has run out. I'm going to destroy you!

My heart dropped. *Why now Sonny*, I thought to myself. We were in the middle of burying my mother-in-law and to see that text instantly made me feel uneasy. I'd been ignoring my phone for a couple of days. For the past week I'd been out of touch with everyone, including Ashley. My wife needed me. Looking at my phone again another text appeared from the same number.

I warned you. How does Gianni feel about having a baby brother?

A sense of relief filled my body. It was Cherry sending empty threats once again. But there was no way I was claiming a baby by her ass. The little boy looked nothing like me or even my daughter for that matter. Breaking from my deep thought, I was interrupted by the love of my life.

"Daddy, is Nana up in the sky with the white birds?" Gianni asked.

"Yes, baby. She's up in heaven with God and the doves."

"Charles, have them bring the car around. We're ready to head to the house now for the repast," I said to my assistant, as I picked up my daughter and ushered my wife from the lawn of the church where the white dove ceremony took place.

"Thank you so much for being here, Malcolm," Charlotte whispered. I could see her pain in her face even though she tried to hide behind her oversized Oliver Peoples sunglasses.

"No matter what we are going through, your mom was like a mother to me. Furthermore, she was an amazing grandmother to Gianni," I responded.

Charlotte's mom had finally lost her battle against cancer, and I felt terrible about it. They were best friends, so it was important that we put our differences aside and to be there for her. Making love to Charlotte the other day may have been a bad idea, but I tried to do all I could to help take her pain away. Since we had sex, she'd been a lot easier to deal with. I didn't know if it was the vulnerability of losing her mom or the sex, but she wasn't as bitter as usual.

My life was so crazy right now. Half the time I didn't know if I was coming or going. Ashley had been calling me nonstop all week, but I hadn't gotten back to her. Somehow, I had to make a way to let her know I was gonna get with her soon. She was my new investment and I'd put too much time and energy into the reality show to let it fall by the wayside. But eventually we would have to be just friends. I cared for Ashley deeply, but after that whole ordeal with Cherry, I was starting to wonder if my affairs were really worth my family. With the mob on my back and my wife's recent loss, I really needed to stay under the radar and tend to what was most important.

Once we got in the car, I checked my messages from earlier this week.

Message 1- Malcolm, why aren't you returning my calls? I understand your wife's mom died, but what does that have to do with us?

Message 2- Malcolm, call me, I miss you?

Message 3- Malcolm, it's Cherry. I'm sorry for what I did, but I needed to get your attention. Call me. Please. MJ needs you.

Where the hell are my aspirin, I mumbled while fumbling through my suit jacket pocket.

My chest pains were on a regular with all the drama in my life. Cherry had sold her story to the tabloids. With me dodging death daily, I was beyond stressed out. I tried to over power Charlotte with affection so that she would be shielded from the most recent paparazzi drama with Cherry. It was easy to convince her that Cherry was doing all this for publicity. But whether Charlotte believed me or not, she'd been numb lately to the outside world. Drama was an afterthought and really didn't seem to matter right now.

As we rode back to the house, the constant vibration of my cell phone became quite annoying. If I could've taken a quick peak at my phone without Charlotte knowing, that would've made things a lot easier. However, to avoid conflict, I decided waiting would be the wiser thing to do.

Once we arrived back at home, and I made sure Charlotte was in the hands of family, I went to the study to see who'd been calling my phone constantly. This time it was from a private number.

"Hello."

"Malcolm, you finally answered. I was in the emergency room all night with your son and I needed you. Ever since you've been involved with that stripper chick you've been giving me the cold shoulder."

"Cherry, this isn't the right time. I just buried my daughter's grandmother," I whispered in a harsh tone.

"Dammit, Malcolm I will not be ignored! I don't deserve this shit. For the past two years I've dealt with your wife harassing me and I've played the perfect sidepiece. Now, when I need you the most you aren't there. I don't deserve this!" Cherry yelled.

"And I don't deserve your lack of respect of what my family is going through right now. Besides, why should I believe that this boy is my son, Cherry? We've always used protection. Why would I believe you? Why now? Who even knows if he's your son? How could you hide a pregnancy from me? You're just desperate for attention!"

"Desperate, Malcolm? You've gotta be kidding me. Yes, I loved you and I'm hurt by the way you're treating me, but there's no way I would concoct a story that wasn't true. If that were the case, I would've pinned him on my ex. He's a football player with millions."

"Who just got cut, might I add. Who do you think you're fooling? And you should be ashamed of yourself naming that child after me," I whispered again angrily. "Now, stop calling me before I get a restraining order on your pressed ass."

"If I have to stake out in front of your fucking house until I get you to understand my son needs you I will. Go ahead and get the restraining order drawn up because I'm not going anywhere! Trust me!" she yelled before I hung up on her.

Turning my phone off, I exited my study and bumped right into Charlotte, who immediately broke down in tears.

"Malcolm, I don't think I'm going to make it without my mom. I just can't."

"Baby, it's okay. You have me. We'll get through this together," I tried to console.

"But it hurts. It hurts bad," Charlotte said, burying her head in my chest.

I rubbed my wife's back. "It's gonna be okay. I promise."

It took Charlotte a while, but she finally got herself together so she could make her way through the rest of the many family members giving hugs and handshakes. Charlotte's family would love if I wasn't there for her, but there was no way I was gonna prove them right. Avoiding my father-in-law was impossible after a while. Midway through the repast, it was inevitable that we would have to exchange words. The way he walked through my home as if he was the man of the house annoyed me in itself. Just when I tried to avoid him for the umpteenth time, his loud boisterous voice called out my name.

"Malcom!"

I did a quick head nod.

"So, Malcolm, tell me what mess you've gotten yourself into now?"

I sighed. "And how are you today, Mr. Madison?"

"You don't give a damn about how I'm doing, and I damn sure could give a baboon's ass about you. Let's cut the crap. Anytime my daughter asks me for a large sum of money, then I know it's to bail your sorry ass out of some kind of mess. My daughter is too good for you. She should've stuck with that other fellow Carl, he's on his way to becoming a judge, you know. You don't realize you have a gem. You're constantly embarrassing my wife in the media and I'm tired of all your damn shenanigans."

"With all do respect sir…" I tried to say.

"What do you know about respect? That word should be removed from your vocabulary."

"Mr. Madison, this is not the time or place to discuss what goes on in my household. Let's get through this tough day with Charlotte and then we can discuss any issues we have like men over a drink or something."

"I wouldn't dare share the same table with scum like you."

Charlotte walked up just in time. Saved by the bell.

"Malcolm, where is Gianni?"

I shrugged my shoulders. "I thought she was with you. Where's my security?"

The first thing that came to mind was that bastard Sonny. Did they get to my daughter? I panicked as we split up to look for Gianni. After looking in her room and her favorite hiding spot, all of a sudden I heard my wife let out a piercing scream. But it wasn't a scream of fear. It was anger. As I made my way back into the foyer, I noticed the scream had come from the downstairs bathroom. There was a man that I'd never seen before holding my daughter. With Gianni's panties down to her legs, rage and anger took over my body.

"Daddy, I needed help wiping myself. I'm sorry," Gianni apologized. I stood paralyzed with anger.

"Get your filthy hands off my daughter. How dare you show your face here?" Charlotte had a look of fear and anger rolled up in one as she snatched Gianni from his arms.

"Charlotte, calm your nerves. She was asking for help, so I helped her," the older man replied.

"Uncle Harry, you better not ever touch my daughter again, you filthy bastard!" Charlotte ran over to Gianni and pulled her panties up before pulling her away.

"Listen, I'm here to pay respect to my baby sister. Now, is that any way to talk to your Uncle Harry? It's been years, come give me a hug," he said with open arms.

Charlotte put up her hand. "You selfish bastard. You disgust me. I would never let you touch me again!"

As Charlotte shook uncontrollably, Gianni started to get upset. We were all confused by her actions.

"Why are you talking to your Uncle this way?" Mr. Madison questioned.

"Daddy, he's a pig and I want him gone. Now!"

There were more than two hundred people in our home and the louder my wife became the more people gathered around.

"Baby, are you okay? What's wrong? Who are these people?" I inquired.

Charlotte pointed. "That's my disgusting Uncle Harry and his wife, Tina."

"What's wrong with you? Why are you shaking like this?" I asked.

Tears overcame Charlotte's face once again. "He took my virginity when I was twelve years old, that's why."

"He what?" Mr. Madsion interjected.

"Malcolm, this is why I've been such a mess. All of this has been bottled up inside. I've hidden this secret all these

years. All these years I wondered, why me," Charlotte continued to cry.

"Why do you people continue to lie on me?" Harry
butted in with a smug tone.

There was so much anger and nervousness that filled my
body, I was ready to unload on the first person that took me
over the edge. His arrogance was unbearable and the way his
wife held his arm as if she wasn't a bit fazed infuriated me even
more. Just when I reached over to knock his ass out, a loud ex-
plosion sounded in my driveway. All of the glass in the front of
my house shattered and everybody ran for cover. When I looked
up there were razors and nails all in the wall.

Oh my God, a nail bomb, I whispered to myself.

"Gianni, where are you?" I yelled while trying to deci-
pher through the smoke.

"I have her. She's over here with me!" Charlotte called
out.

"What the hell was that?" someone yelled out.

"It seemed to be a car bomb!" another screamed while
several other people coughed uncontrollably.

"Is everyone alright?" I yelled before going outside.
There was so much chaos going on with people running in all
directions.

Just when I was about to go back inside to check on my
wife and daughter, I heard tires screech, pulling away in a
hurry. It was Sharrod, Sonny's hit man. I couldn't make out
who else was in the car. It was confirmation that my days were
numbered. As I ran back in the house, I heard my wife screaming and sobbing uncontrollably.

"Oh my God, Daddy! My Daddy. My Daddy!" Charlotte
cried.

Mr. Madison was on the floor with a large piece of glass
lodged into his chest. The razors and nails from the bomb that
were plunged in his head were hard to see. Within seconds, the
mob had taken Mr. Madison's life right before my eyes on the

day we'd buried his wife. It was obvious that my bill had to be paid today. I didn't want to be next. My family had to get out of town as soon as possible.

Kennedi-19

Boom, boom.

"What the hell was that?" I yelled after making a right turn onto Malcolm's street.

Whatever it was shook my car, which scared me half to death. California was known for their earthquakes, and I prayed to God that wasn't the case.

I was supposed to be on my way to work, but that reality show could wait. No natural disaster was going to stop me from getting answers on why he'd been ignoring me for over a week. The one time I opened up to a man and fell in love, I got let down. It was important that I spoke to him in person, especially after the morning I had. He needed to know our future was about to change drastically.

With all of the things I'd been hearing in the media with this Cherry chick, it made me wonder if she was telling the truth that night when we were at dinner; which was another reason why he needed to be confronted.

I figured going to his house shouldn't be an issue since his wife knew about us. With all the drama going on with Malcolm, I came prepared with my gun to scare off his wife if need be. If she jumped out there like some kind of bad ass, she was gonna get pistol whipped.

Right as I pulled up at his iron gate there was complete chaos. People were yelling and running in every direction with looks of devastating fear on each of their faces. Church hats were flying off of elderly women's heads as they urgently tried to flee as fast as they could. As I watched the front of Malcolm's house in flames, I wondered what the hell was going on. All of a sudden sirens sounded. As I sat at the bottom of the hill I asked the first lady coming in my direction, what was going on.

"Ma'am, is everything okay? What happened?"

"It's a bomb! It's a bomb!" She seemed terrified while running away.

A bomb, I thought. *Oh my God, I hope Malcolm is alright*. He was all I had, and I needed him at a time like this. Just as I parked, I got the shock of my life when a familiar face stopped me dead in my tracks. *There's no way*, I said to myself, as my heart seemed to take a nosedive to the pit of my stomach.

Blinking my eyes to make sure I wasn't seeing things, I refocused once again. It was really him. What the hell was Sharrod doing out of jail? How did he get out? Even though I hadn't seen him in over two years, I could spot that ugly scar on the side of his face from a mile away. How the hell was this happening? What was he up to and why was he here? Was he after me?

So many questions and thoughts crossed my mind as I watched him peel out in a tinted Suburban. He was with some Italian looking older man. I was convinced he was responsible for this. Why did he do this? Was he trying to send me a message? He was up to no good and I needed to follow him. Maybe he told Malcolm about my secret past? My mind continued to wonder just before I broke from my daze and sprung into action.

Just as I backed up to turn the car around, I was paralyzed with shock once again. A familiar voice that haunted me in my dreams suddenly resonated. That annoying voice was so distinct that it gave me an instant chill throughout my body.

"Come on, woman, hurry up! We gotta get the fuck outta here. These folks are crazy."

"I'm running as fast as I can, don't leave me, dammit!"

It was Harry and Tina Johnson. I hadn't seen them since the day I was brutally attacked and raped as a child. My skin crawled as I flashed back to our last encounter. *What were they doing here*, I thought.

As bad as I wanted to just shoot off rounds at them, I had to be smart. There were police everywhere and this could be my only chance at revenge. Today was the day that they would pay. As bad as I wanted to see what Sharrod was up to, it had to wait for now.

Ducking down in my car, I waited for them to pull off. My stomach was all of a sudden full of butterflies. Suddenly nauseous, I quickly leaned over toward the passenger's seat and threw up my breakfast all over the floor.

"Get yourself together, Kennedi, it's now or never," I said to myself.

I'd been feeling sick more than usual lately, but the sight of Harry and Tina bought back memories that left my stomach unsettled.

As they pulled away from Malcolm's estate, I trailed behind them. It looked as if they were in a heated discussion. Harry had aged a great deal and Tina's once size six hourglass figure had become a size eighteen or twenty easily. I wondered if they were now living in L.A. But more importantly, how did they know Malcolm?

After trailing them for a good half hour with a little traffic, we were in Beverly Hills. As I turned onto Wilshire Blvd., I thought back to Malcolm and prayed he wasn't hurt. They were staying at The Beverly Hills Plaza Hotel, where they were both going to die today.

In guerilla mode, I put on my baseball cap, parked on the street and jumped out. As they pulled up to valet taking their old ass time, I listened to Harry give out the room number, 525 as he rudely snatched his claim ticket from the valet guy. You could tell he was drunk as he stumbled.

Sneaking past them with my gun at my waist, I made it up to the fifth floor like a trained assassin without being noticed. As soon as I approached the room, a deceitful smile invaded my face as I saw the housekeeping cart right outside the door.

This shit is too easy, I thought to myself. It was like fate.

"Is somebody there?" the cleaning lady yelled out as I snuck into the closet while she cleaned the bathroom.

After patiently waiting over fifteen minutes in that stuffy closet, I was closer to getting my revenge. This was the moment I dreamt of all my life. Finally, I heard Tina and Harry's voices as the door opened. I held onto my gun tight.

"You gonna answer me, Harry Johnson. Why did Kasey call your phone this morning? How did she know we were in town? You probably fucking her," Tina said.

"She wants more money for China and I ain't giving her another dime."

"You better not!" Tina yelled.

"I'm gonna get my daughter from them people. Kennedi never wanted that girl and kept her a secret. I'ma get her and treat her right. She needs to be with her Daddy. Seeing her every other couple of months acting like I'm her uncle ain't fair to me. She needs to know!" Harry slurred raising his voice.

My heart was broken. How could Kasey allow China to be around Harry with all he'd done to me? Were my sister and Big Mama that fucking money hungry? Tears flooded from my eyes. This was all my fault.

Trying to maintain my composure, I listened to Harry calm Tina down and talk her into taking a bath with him. She was such an idiot to stay with him all these years. She would believe anything he said and it was sickening. Bitches like her fucked up the world.

"I love you, Harry."

Hearing them kiss as if they didn't have a care in the world made my blood boil. I could no longer contain myself as

I sweated profusely. Slowly opening the closet door, I crept to the bathroom with the gun pointed toward the two people who'd ruined my life.

"What the hell?" Harry yelled. The sight of his body made me sick.

"Oh my God!" Tina screamed as soon as she saw me.

"Shut the fuck up! Both of you! Don't say another word." Tears continued to run down my face as I faced the two people I hated the most.

"Kennedi, look how you've grown. I see you in the papers but, you…"

Before Harry could open his nasty mouth to say another word, I struck him with the gun. Blood gushed from his nose and mouth.

"Shut the fuck up Harry, you drunk bastard. What are you doing here?" I yelled.

"Ouch, you busted my damn nose," Harry whined.

"Kennedi, can you please put the gun down?" Tina pleaded.

"Fuck you, Tina. Answer my question, Harry. What are you doing here? Why were you at my boyfriend's house?"

He held his mouth. "What the hell are you talking about? Who is your boyfriend?"

"Malcolm. Now, tell me what you told him. Why are you here?" I questioned with the gun still pointed.

"Tell him what? It's nothing to tell," Harry replied. "I'm here because I buried my sister today. Malcolm is my niece's husband. Here I am mourning my baby sister, and you holding a damn gun to me."

In disbelief, I stood in shock not knowing what to do next. Moving to California to escape my past was harder than I could ever imagine. How could this world be this small?

Harry wiped some of the blood with the back of his hand. "So, why didn't you ever tell me about China? She looks just like me. We coulda raised her together."

"What do you mean, Harry? I beg your pardon," Tina interrupted.

Grabbing the remote with my gun still directed at them, I raised the volume. Too bad *In Living Color* wasn't on. That would've made everything perfect. While Harry and Tina went back and forth a bit, I wondered how Kasey could do such a thing?

How could she expose China to that bastard?

The more he spoke, the more deranged thoughts filled my mind. I didn't know how I wanted to kill him at the moment, but what I knew for sure was Harry Johnson wasn't gonna ever hurt anyone again. His voice irritated me. His scent made me even sicker. Tina sat there as Harry rambled on and on.

"Don't ever say her name out your mouth again, you fucking pervert. You will never see my daughter again!" I belted.

That was the first time I'd ever said it out loud. At the end of the day China was mine, and I didn't want a scum like Harry to be anywhere around her. I was so emotional.

"I'ma get custody of my daughter before she becomes a whore like you. Plus, Kasey and that grandma of yours tryna suck me dry," Harry stated.

"I'll be damned. You won't live to see the day. You both are finally gonna pay for what you did to me!" I roared.

"I made you strong, girl!" Harry yelled back.

My eyes widened.

"Why do you look so surprised?" he continued.

"Are you serious? You scarred me. My life is all fucked up because of you! I hate both of you for beating me and letting me bleed damn near to death. Do you know I was hospitalized for months as I fought for my life that day?"

"Just put the gun down so we can talk," Tina begged.

"Fuck no!" I cried before flashing back again.

My body shook badly while tears poured from my eyes.

Before Harry could say another word, I blacked out and started firing shots. I put two slugs right into Harry's chest just as Tina jumped up. But I sat her fat ass down too with a slug straight in her head. That was the quietest I'd ever seen Harry in my life.

Needing insurance to make sure they were gone for good, I plugged up the blow dryer into the wall. As I dropped it in the tub, I watched those bastards cook. The weight on my heart was lifted. At last, I'd gotten my revenge. Finally, my nightmares were over.

Kennedi-20

Father God in the Name of Jesus, please forgive me, Lord. I'm not a murderer. My heart is heavy and I'm aware that what I did was wrong. Please help guide me to live in your light. Please forgive me father, for I have sinned. Amen

Big Mama used to always say, if you ever do something wrong, just say that prayer and God will forgive you. Of course I had to freestyle it a bit, but God knew my heart. Hopefully the old lady knew what she was talking about because my life was a big mess and it felt like murderer was tattooed across my forehead. Everyday I lived in fear that I would be arrested at any time. I wasn't a killer and I prayed every morning for forgiveness since I killed Ray and Isis. Now, with having to off Harry and Tina that was four bodies under my belt. A part of me wanted to do away with the gun. But now that I knew for sure Sharrod was in L.A. and out of jail, I needed protection.

Sleeping alone hadn't been any fun either. Malcolm still hadn't called me, but he did finally respond to my text letting me know he was okay. Even though I needed to talk to him in person, it was best that I didn't overwhelm him right now. It was all over the news how someone had tried to murder him, but ultimately killed his father-in-law instead, and over a dozen people were injured. Sharrod was obviously out for blood. But what I still couldn't understand was the connection between him and Malcolm. Was he that mad at me? Was he that jealous?

As I drove to the set of the reality show, it was time to

make a phone call to get some information. I knew just who had the answers I was looking for.

"Hello."

"Big Mama."

"Kennedi, is that you?"

"Yeah, it's me," I said softly.

"I'm not feeling up to your bickering right now. Big Mama doesn't feel too good. My arthritis has been bothering me and my sugar is up," she complained as usual looking for sympathy.

"Actually, Big Mama, I didn't call to fuss or argue. I just called to apologize for the way I've been treating you. The way I've neglected my kids. I just want to make things right."

"Really." I could sense her smile through the phone. "Kasey told me you wanted nothing to do with them kids. That poor Chase has been a mess since he's seen you."

"Big Mama, I just wanted a better life for him. I'm doing very well for myself and I want to just be able to share my success with both my children. I'm gonna take care of you too for all you've done over the years. You can come live out here with me once I get my house."

"Chile, I'm not getting on nobody's plane, riding for all them hours. Kasey tried to get me to go with her and Sharrod when they had their...Hold on a second."

She clicked over to the other line. I was dying to know what she was talking about. Just like I thought, she was my ticket to know where to find Sharrod. I had to find him before he got to me. Luckily, he didn't see me at Malcolm's.

"Yes, those damn bill collectors keep calling. I'm not giving them a dime. I ain't got many years left, you know."

"You have plenty time left, Big Mama."

"Nawwww, Suga. I don't."

"Don't say that." I couldn't wait to ask her about Sharrod again, but she kept talking.

"You know I got all kinds of ailments. And..."

I cut her off. "Listen, Big Mama…"

"What is it, baby?"

"So, what you were telling me about Sharrod?"

"He's such a fine fella. He's so good to that Chase," Big Mama praised.

"When's the last time you talked to him?"

"He checks on me everyday. I just hung up with him right before you called. You want me to tell him to call you?"

"No, I'll just go talk to him in person. Do you have his number?" I asked.

"Let me go and get my address book. I think that's a good idea. You know, fixing things with the kids and all. They need their mama. You and Kasey need to make things right, too. Before I go away from here I need you and your sister to bury the hatchet. Life is too short to hold onto grudges. Family should always stick together. Your daddy wouldn't like to see y'all this way."

"You're right," I agreed rolling my eyes in my head.

Before long my grandmother had given me both Sharrod's phone number and address. Older people were so trustworthy and easy to trick.

"Okay, Big Mama. I'ma check on you tomorrow, okay?"

"Alright, chile. God is good. I've been praying on you Kennedi, and He finally answered my prayers. Wait 'til I tell Sister Montgomery."

"Talk to you tomorrow. I love you," I said, rushing her off the phone.

Dumb bitch.

As soon as I got to the set and stepped out of my car, I was bombarded by photographers. What would be the questions today? Luckily security was outside and whisked me into the mansion. As soon as I came in the door, all eyes were on me. Was I just being paranoid or was everybody on the set staring at me crazy this morning.

Neko Luv walked up to me looking concerned. "I need

to holler at you for a minute."

"What's up, Neko?" I said, wondering where the hell he'd found some red True Religion jeans. He always took that gangster shit to another level, which was a complete turn off.

"Have you looked at Media Take Out today?" he asked.

My heart sunk and instantly I felt ill as my paranoia kicked in again. Was that why the paparazzi were outside today? Did someone expose me for killing Isis and Ray? Did someone at the hotel see me leaving after I killed Tina and Harry. But I covered up everything so well.

"No, why?"

"Look," Neko said, pulling out his phone and going straight to the urban gossip app.

The headline read, *Reality Star, Ashley Jacobs of the new show Neko Finds Luv, is a Lezbo Say it Ain't So. Click here to see the video of the sexy stallion.*

There I was with Isis as she had her way with me. It was obvious that I was drunk by how lethargic I seemed. I was humiliated. With Isis dead, I wondered who could've done this to me.

"Who did this, Neko?"

"Man, I don't know. I just thought I would let you know what all the hush was about before we go on set. One of those hatin' chicks might try to call you out. I like you, even though I was ordered not to fall for you. Man, you cool peeps."

"I feel so embarrassed."

"Don't let this shit get you down. I wouldn't be surprised if the producers of the show did that shit on purpose. You know we need ratings when the show comes out. Look at the bright side, Kim K came up from that Ray J shit. Hell, it might work in your favor."

"No, you don't understand," I wailed. "I don't need this shit in my life right now."

"Word. I feel you. But it is what it is."

I had no more words for him. I simply dove my head

into his chest and cried like a newborn baby for nearly five minutes while he fed me bullshit about how things would eventually die down and be forgotten about.

After venting to Neko for a little bit, I realized he was a really nice guy. He might've been a little off base thinking Malcolm had anything to do with the video, but other than that he was cool. It was rare that I spoke to him off camera. I really appreciated him trying to look out for me. We chatted for a good half an hour and before I knew it, we were being called to begin filming for the day.

"Quiet on the set!" someone shouted.

"You ready to do this?" Neko asked in a romantic voice.

I nodded wondering why Neko was eyeballing me like that. I hoped he didn't think our conversation had led to something more.

"Action!" the producer called out a few seconds later.

The producer cued for Neko Luv and I to pick up where we left off with a kiss. He was a cutie, but I just wasn't really into him. The chicks on the show really wanted him, but this was just a come-up for me. I even had to beat a bitch ass on camera the other day. For ratings, I'm sure it was a set up, but I handled my business. The good thing was it was almost all over. It was exciting to know that there was only a few days left of filming.

"I could get used to this everyday," Neko said, staring deep into my eyes.

The scary thing was I didn't think he was no longer acting. It was obvious he was falling for me. As I faked like Neko was the best thing since sliced bread, our production was suddenly cut, by unexpected visitors.

"Is Malcolm Fitzgerald available?" a short Italian man asked.

It was the same guy I saw in the car with Sharrod. I slipped away from the scene and hid far enough to escape if needed, but close enough to not miss a beat. There was no way

I was chancing Sharrod seeing me. I wondered why he was here for Malcolm? Were they looking for me, too? All types of thoughts danced through my head, just before Sharrod appeared with an AK-47 in tow. All hell was about to break loose and fear consumed my body.

"He hasn't been on set in weeks. Did you want to leave him a message?"one of the production assistants asked.

"Yeah," Sharrod answered right before letting off a shot right in his chest.

Everyone started screaming.

"What the fuck?" Neko yelled.

Before he could take a step, Sharrod sprayed him down. Neko Luv never had a chance. He was dead. Sharrod was trying to kill everything in sight as he let off round after round destroying any and everything he could.

The girls ran for their lives. I watched a few die right on the spot. My heart thumped. As I hid behind the sauna, I watched Sharrod and two other guys destroy all of the camera equipment. They even shot fire at the columns in the foyer, which caused the entire staircase and balcony to collapse. Debris fell all over me and I laid there under it all making sure not to make a sound.

"Come on, Sharrod, let's go before the cops get here," the Italian man ordered.

"Not yet," Sharrod responded. "I can smell her. I know she's here."

"Who? Sharrod, let's go," the short man ordered again.

There was no doubt the entire mansion was destroyed. From the camera men to the props, the room was full of smoke. As soon as I heard them exiting in a hurry, Sharrod spoke.

"Kennedi, you're next!"

I was determined to escape the mansion alive and before the police arrived. Once the coast was clear, I ran to my car in top speed and pulled off. As I cried like a baby, I shook nervously peeking in my rearview mirror every few seconds. I called and texted Malcolm a million times to tell him what happened. But there was still no response. It was the grace of God that allowed me to make it home alive. As soon as I got in the house, I finally felt safe. Trying to call Malcolm again there was no answer. Suddenly, I heard someone approach the door. It was probably Malcolm. I ran to the door and opened it when suddenly everything went dark.

Malcolm-21

"The accounts are frozen? You've got to be kidding me, Charlotte!" I panicked while driving my wife and daughter to the airport. There was no way I would let another day go by putting their lives at risk.

"There is an investigation in progress to rule out foul play with Daddy's death before releasing the funds. It can take weeks."

"Charlotte, I don't have weeks. These people are trying to kill me."

"You think I don't know that. My father was killed because of your bullshit. This is all your fault! You're the reason why I have to pull my daughter out of school and go stay with my cousins in Chicago. I can't even mourn my father's death because you're so hell bent on getting money."

"I know, and I'm truly sorry about all this Charlotte. I feel horrible. Now that you know how serious this situation is, I don't understand why you refuse to travel with my security. I don't know what I would do if I lost you, let alone Gianni."

"I'm not gonna live my life in fear because of your mishaps, Malcolm. And now you're sorry. Sorry about what? Where shall you begin with your damn apologies?" Charlotte waited for a few seconds. "Answer me!"

My wife was right. I had put her through so much and was at a loss for words. I didn't know how to fix what had been set in motion. Looking at Gianni sleeping through the rearview mirror, I tried to swallow the lump that had formed in my throat. There was no way I could imagine life without her and had to get this Sonny situation under control, pronto.

As I approached the United Airlines terminal, I got emotional. After placing my car in park, I looked over at my wife. The thought of not seeing my family ever again scared me. Would Sonny get to me before I joined them in Chicago? He constantly haunted my thoughts.

"Charlotte, we'll get through this. I promise."

Before she could respond, we were hit slightly from behind by another vehicle and my car jerked.

"What the hell was that?" Charlotte yelled.

Instantly, my heart dropped. Were Sonny and his goons here to finish me off? As I gazed through my side mirror, I saw an hourglass figure quickly sashay to my side of the car with a baby in tow. It was Cherry.

"So, I have to stake out in front of your house and follow you in order to get your attention," she spat.

"Cherry, this is not a good time." I tried my best to use a smooth tone to keep her calm as well.

"Well, when is a good time, Malcolm? You will not continue to ignore me and your son."

"Your son!" Charlotte couldn't unbuckle her seatbelt fast enough. "Malcolm, this is it. I'm taking my daughter to Chicago and filing for divorce. No more! I will not stand for any more of this!" Charlotte yelled as she grabbed Gianni from the backseat.

"Mommy, where are we going?" Gianni asked, puzzled waking up from her deep sleep.

"We're leaving. Your father has put me through enough," Charlotte mumbled as she grabbed her purse.

"Charlotte, wait a minute. You're gonna leave me because of some groupie bitch lying on me?"

"Groupie? Is that how you treat the mother of your only son?" Cherry countered.

"That's not my son!" I yelled.

"I'm done, Malcom!" Charlotte said, slamming the door. She was in such a hurry to leave she forgot their luggage in the trunk.

"Sir, you're gonna have to move your vehicle!" the airport police officer ordered.

"I hope you're fucking satisfied," I said, looking at Cherry with disgust right before pulling off.

No matter what we went through over the years, Charlotte had never mentioned divorce. She was finally fed up. I could see it in her eyes. However, Charlotte being upset with me had to be put on the back burner for now. The most important thing was getting her and Gianni out of California. As soon as they landed in Chicago safely, I would call and try to smooth things over.

As I drove away from the airport, my adrenaline pumped with nervousness. With my mind heavier than a Sumo wrestler, I needed to decompress for a minute, so I decided to turn on the radio. Just what I needed, flashback Friday and my favorite love song *Wildflower* by New Birth was on. Every time I heard that song, it reminded me of my wife when we were really in love. As soon as my favorite part came on, my mood was immediately ruined by the interruption by the DJ.

"We're sorry to interrupt, but we have breaking news. Rapper Neko Luv was gunned down earlier today while taping his reality show that was set to air this summer. Sources say there were five other fatalities and seven others injured. At this time, police do not have any suspects, and…"

In a state of shock I searched for my phone in the console. That explained why my shit had been vibrating off the hook all morning and afternoon. To ease Charlotte's nerves, I'd turned my ringer off to avoid another argument, but now I regretted that decision. The amount of text messages and voicemails I had were insane.

Message 1

*Man, nigga, what the fuck kinda shit you involved in?
My nigga Neko Luv is dead. Hit me up ASAP!*

Message 2

*Malcolm, the set just got shot up and I'm scared to
death. I need you. I'm driving home now scared shitless. Some
Italian guy came to the set threatening your life. I'm scared,
Malcolm. Please meet me at home.*

There were plenty more messages, but those two had
summed everything up perfectly. Sonny had struck again. As
soon as I made it off the 405 freeway, I jumped on I-10 and
headed straight to the penthouse to get my money and get out of
town. I felt awful. Lives were being destroyed all around me
and there was nothing I could do about it. There was no way I
could pay the bill on my head, so I had to roll.

It was hard to believe that another business venture I'd
invested in shot straight to hell. My luck was the worst. I just
couldn't get it right. Now, there was another meal ticket gone,
and another group of investors I'd pissed off. However, not only
was tons of money about to be lost, but Donovan had lost his
artist and a close friend.

Once I arrived at the penthouse, I was on a mission to
get the hell out of town. There was no way Ashley could stay
either. Until I figured shit out, she would just have to stay in a
hotel or something. I definitely didn't want her to be next.

"Ashley, come on we gotta get outta here!" I yelled as
soon as I walked in. "Ashley, where are you?"

Paranoid as hell, I locked the door and went straight to
my daughter's portrait.

I love you Gianni, I whispered before moving the picture, preparing to enter my safe. It was imperative that I got my
rainy day stash before I headed to Chicago. It was no telling
when I was gonna be back in L.A. The hard part was breaking
the news to Ashley.

Now that the reality show set had been shot up and the
star of the show was killed, my Plan B for getting paid was de-

stroyed. To make matters worse, Neko was a Blood, so I would have to answer to that shit as well. His crew had already left a message wanting answers.

Running up to the bedroom, I called out for Ashley again. I couldn't believe my eyes. Was she crazy? There she was sprawled across the bed naked.

"I missed you, Malcolm," she said, rubbing between her legs.

"Ashley, get up! We gotta go. Someone is trying to kill me and all you can think about is getting fucked. Our lives are in danger and I need to get the hell out of here."

"I knew you were gonna be all tense, so I made you a drink," she responded unenthused.

"Why the hell are you talking about a drink when you know what's going on? Weren't you the one telling me how scared you were earlier? Weren't you there when my fucking set was ruined?" I asked before walking over to my nightstand. The first thing I had to grab was my watch collection.

"Malcolm, just drink this. I'll help you pack. Let me take care of you for a change."

The way Ashley acted had me concerned. I knew she'd grown up rough, but it bothered me that sex was on her mind after damn near being killed today.

Snatching the glass of Merlot from her, I gulped it down and sat on the bed to try and collect my thoughts. I was at a loss of what to do next. How did my life turn into this?

"Malcolm, I'm sorry things are going haywire in your life right now. But I'm here for you. Now, kiss me."

"No, I gotta…"

"Malcolm, just kiss me."

No longer could I fight the temptation. I had to have her. Within seconds, something came over me and made me want to be inside of her. As soon as the blood rushed to the tip of my dick, it was no turning back. No matter how bad my mind told me to fight Ashley off and get the hell out of dodge, my manhood told me something different. As she bent over and allowed me to enter her ass, I thrust deep inside of somewhere she'd never let me before. Today Ashley was different. It was if she had something to prove. No longer did I have control. My body felt as if I was floating on air as I thrust a few times.

"I'm about to cum!"

Suddenly, she moved up, causing my dick to fall out. "No, don't cum yet. We're not done." After pulling me onto the bed, it wasn't long before Ashley climbed on top. "Now, it's time for me to ride this big dick," she said, fucking me hard.

Was there something in that drink was all I could think. I could no longer talk. What the hell did she give me? I went from being horny to defenseless. As she bounced on my dick like a Texas cowgirl, I watched her breast jump up and down until my eyes got heavy. Finally, beyond my control I could no longer see Ashley. She disappeared right before my eyes.

Kennedi-22

"Ouch, what the hell? Where am I? What just happened?" I said, trying to make out my bearings before realizing I was trapped in what appeared to be a closet.

How the hell did I get in here? Where was Malcolm? Was Sharrod behind this? All types of questions invaded my thoughts. Even though I felt groggy, I needed to escape. As I stood up from the floor, I also felt a little dizzy, but nothing was about to stop me from getting out of the tight space. I'd never felt so claustrophobic in my life. Feeling for the knob, I tried to turn it repeatedly and push the door open, but it was stuck. It was obvious that something was on the other side and had me trapped. After quickly thinking of another plan, I laid down on the floor and started kicking with every ounce of strength I had left. It took a few tries, but moments later, the door opened, sending a chair flying across the room.

The crazy thing was, instead of me being in some type of deserted house like I first thought; I was still in Malcolm's penthouse. Rubbing the side of my temple, I tried to recall how I ended up in the coat closet in the first place, and why the person responsible attempted to lock me in there. I had no idea what the fuck was going on. Looking at my watch, I realized it was only 6 o'clock in the evening. It felt like midnight.

"Malcolm, Malcolm. Where are you?" I said, running upstairs to our bedroom. "Oh my God, Malcolm!"

I screamed at what stood before me. There was no way

this was happening. How could he do this to me?

"What the hell is going on? Malcolm, how could you?"

My heart dropped at the sight of my man under the covers with a female. All I saw was a heap of curly hair with him passed out beside her. As soon as I yanked the covers back, I heard the voice I detested the most. I couldn't believe that bitch had stooped so low.

"Guess you woke up from your nap, huh?"

Kasey was in bed with the love of my life.

Instantly, my memory came back and I recalled her being at the door not Malcolm. Looking at Malcolm out of it, I didn't know what to think. He was in a deep slumber.

"You desperate whore!" I yelled, going straight into attack mode.

"Kennedi, what's your problem? You liked sharing before," Kasey said right before I flung her naked body onto the floor.

All I saw was red and I wanted her dead. As we rolled across the floor holding each other's hair, Malcolm finally came to.

"Hey…what the hell is going on?" he questioned groggily while rubbing his head.

"Bitch, I'ma kill you!" I said, trying to ram my sister's head straight into the mahogany wooded floors.

We were going for blows when Malcolm stumbled, making it out of the bed. It hurt to see them both naked. Moments later, he was finally able to get in between us. It seemed like forever before Malcolm could unlock Kasey's hair from between my fingers.

"Malcolm, how could you? You said you would never hurt me," I cried.

"She must've drugged me, baby," he responded.

"Awww, it's no need to lie, Malcolm. I don't have to drug men in order to get dick," Kasey instigated.

At that moment, Malcolm looked back and forth between me and my sister several times before rubbing his eyes. "Hold up. Is this your twin, that you were telling me about? Her name is Kennedi, right?"

Kasey laughed. "Is that what she told you? No dear, my name is Kasey. Mr. Fitzgerald, your girlfriend is Kennedi." She stared at me. "Bitch, you're good."

"Ashley, what the hell is going on?" Malcolm questioned.

"Her name is Kennedi!" Kasey felt the need to say.

I shook my head. "She's lying, Malcolm."

"Look, I don't have time for this shit! Now, tell me the truth. Who the hell are you woman?" Malcolm was furious.

It was no need to continue with the lie any further. It was obvious that I wasn't gonna be able to get out of this one. "My name is Kennedi Kramer and I..."

"And she has two kids that she left behind for me to take care of while she was in jail for two years," Kasey interrupted.

It looked like Malcolm could kill me. "Guess my wife was right about you all along."

"Yeah, she was," Kasey added.

"Shut the hell up, Kasey! I hate you. All you ever wanted to do was sabotage my life. Why Kasey? Why are you so hell bent on destroying me? What did I ever do to make you hate me so much?"

"You never gave me a chance at life. From the day you fucked Harry I hated you," she fired back.

"He raped me, Kasey!" I roared.

"But you let him! You let him fuck you. He didn't hold a gun to your head."

"Why did you let him see China, he's a pedophile?"

"Sharrod was right. All you care about is Kennedi. Fuck your son; the hell with your daughter. It's all about Kennedi," Kasey said.

"Fuck you and Sharrod! You're not gonna come here and destroy my life. You'll die before I let you do that," I said right before hog spitting in Kasey's face. I despised that desperate bitch and wanted her dead.

Suddenly Malcolm's eyes grew wider. "Sharrod? How do you know him?"

"That's our baby daddy. We both have sons by him." Kasey looked at me with a little smirk. "The nephew that you always called a faggot is Sharrod's son, too. We've been fucking for years," Kasey taunted as she slipped her dress on.

"Both of you bitches are crazy. Get the fuck out of my house! You were working with him all along?" Malcolm pointed in my direction. "You set me up!"

"Malcolm, what are you talking about?" I asked.

"You must've moved here to set me up. I can't believe I fell for you. You're nothing but a thirsty slut. Get the fuck outta my house, now!" Malcolm was furious.

"You can't leave me, Malcolm. You are all I have. I need you, I'm pregnant," I tried to inform.

"And I don't give a fuck. Now, get out my house before I call the cops and have you thrown out. I never want to see your face again!" he responded with a cold tone.

"Guess my work is done here," Kasey added before leaving out of the room.

While she walked away satisfied, I sat there on the floor for a moment paralyzed in shock. I couldn't believe what had just happened. When I heard the door slam downstairs, something clicked in me. There was no way Kasey could've devised this plan alone. It was time to follow her and see what else she and Sharrod were up to.

"Ashley, Kennedi, or whoever the fuck you are; this is the last time I tell you nicely to get out of my house." Malcolm grabbed me by my arm and forced me out of his room and down the steps. He was hurt and I hated Kasey more than ever for inflicting this pain.

"I heard you Malcolm, but you have to believe that I'm sorry."

"Sorry. So, you help your child's father set me up by pretending to love me, and all you can say is sorry? Fuck you."

I walked towards the door, opened it, and then stepped outside. "I don't know what's going on with you and Sharrod, but I had nothing to do with it. I'm carrying your child, so I would never do anything like that. You're not getting rid of me that easy."

"How convenient? Now, all of sudden you're pregnant."

"That's what I've been trying to talk to you about, but you were so wrapped up in your wife's ass, that you didn't have the time to see what was going on with me. I could've died today. Would you have even cared? Did you ever really care about me, or was the girl Cherry right about you?"

"Don't you dare try and flip everything on me! I trusted you and look what you did. I thought you were different, but you're no different from any other groupie who tried to get in my pockets for a damn come up. Now, get the fuck off my doormat!"

"I will be back."

"And I won't be here," Malcolm said, before slamming the door in my face.

My life had just gone from sugar to shit in a blink of an eye. Why was I experiencing all this bad karma? Was it because of how I treated my kids? Was it because I destroyed Malcolm's marriage? My conscience was getting the best of me. Eventually, I knew I needed to make things right with both Chase and China, but for now it was time to make Kasey pay.

Taking the short cut to the underground parking structure, I spotted her texting on her phone with a huge grin on her face. She had no clue I was on to her. As I followed her out of the parking lot she also had no idea I was right behind her.

Thinking of everything that had just gone down, my heart began to hurt. I couldn't believe that Sharrod was my nephew's father. While everyone always made me out to be this horrible person, apparently my sister was being just as deceitful the entire time. Big Mama probably knew, too. Everyone had betrayed me. The only thing in my life that made me feel like I had a chance was Malcolm. Now, he wanted nothing to do with me.

As I followed Kasey on I-10, I wondered where she was off to now. There were so many questions that filled my mind. What was Sharrod and Malcolm's connection? Just when I thought Sharrod ruined my reality show to get back at me, he had an even bigger beef with Malcolm. Who was the Italian guy Sharrod was with and what did he want with Malcolm? That was the same dude at Malcolm's house the day of the bombing. It was a big piece of the puzzle missing and I was going to get to the bottom of everything today.

Getting into guerrilla mode, my blood boiled. The more I watched Kasey drive the white Porsche Cayenne truck in front of me, the more pissed off I became. Sharrod was really taking care of her. Revenge and anger filled my spirit as I stayed focused glancing at the gun on my lap. My pain was all her fault. She would never hurt me again. Now, it was payback time.

Malcolm-23

Finally, I'd got those crazy fraudulent bitches out of my house. I should've known that wasn't Ashley when the trick let me go straight in her ass. *How could I be such a fool? That bitch was playing me the whole time,* I thought to myself before throwing the last bit of things into my luggage.

How was it that I didn't see the signs before? Her real name was Kennedi. That explained the K heart S tattoo that was on the small of her back. I couldn't believe that I'd treated my wife like shit while sleeping with the enemy this entire time. I had to admit, I'd fallen in love, but couldn't really say the same for her. Who knew if the pain in her eyes were real?

The more I thought about it, I couldn't believe I'd allowed myself to fall for someone I knew nothing about. Why did I allow her in my home so quick? I was Malcolm Fitzgerald, how did I fall for such a low life/ So many regrets filled my thoughts. I had such a great wife and now I could've possibly fathered two children outside of my marriage. My life couldn't possibly get any worse. I had so many unanswered questions, but no time to spend another second thinking about it. My life was in danger and I had to get out of town…fast.

Grabbing my phone off the bed, I called Charlotte to see if she and my daughter had arrived in Chicago safely. When there was no answer, I decided to leave her a message.

Baby. I'm so sorry for continuously hurting you. I know you may not believe this but, there's no way I will ever hurt you again. My life is purposeless without you in it and I promise I'm gonna do all I can for the rest of my life, proving to you that you mean the world to me. We can't get a divorce. We just can't.

My last resort to get in touch with Charlotte was Charles, so I called his number next.

"Hello."

"Charles."

"Yes, Malcolm, what do you want?" he answered annoyed. By the tone in his voice, I'm sure Charlotte had called and told him everything that happened right before her plane took off.

"Have you heard from Charlotte yet?" Lord knows I didn't want to call Charles, but I knew that if my wife would've contacted anyone once she arrived in Chicago, it would be him.

"No, Malcolm. She was supposed to have landed by now, and hasn't been answering the phone."

"Shit!"

"What have you done now?"

Maybe he doesn't know what happened, I thought. "We kind of had a bit of drama at the airport with Cherry."

"Cherry? Malcolm, when are you going to learn? This heffer drags your name through the tabloids for a check claiming you're the father of her child and you still choose to sleep with her. Haven't you hurt Charlotte enough? When will you ever learn? Charlotte is too good for you!"

"You don't even know what happened. Fuck it, Charles. I don't need to hear any shit from you right now," I said, right before hanging up on him.

My mind raced while paranoia took over my body. I just needed to hear Charlotte's voice. There was no way I was going to give her a divorce. I wanted my family back and would do anything I needed to in order to make things right.

My chest started bothering me again, so I popped another Aspirin right before I took my luggage downstairs. It was weird to me that I hadn't gotten any calls from Sharrod or

Sonny all day. After I sent him the message letting him know our accounts were frozen and I would get him the money from my father-in-law's estate maybe he decided to give me a break. Hopefully, that was the case. In the meantime, I just needed to get to my family.

Glancing up at the life size photo of Gianni in the foyer, I was ready to leave when there was a loud knock at the door. Hopefully, I hadn't spoken too soon.

"Mr. Fitzgerald, this is the LAPD. Open up!" a loud male voice called out.

Police? What the hell do they want, I wondered.

Looking through the peephole to make sure it was really the cops, I saw two white officers with military style haircuts at my door. When it dawned on me that my neighbors had probably called them again because of all the drama that had just taken place, I opened the door relieved that it wasn't Sonny or one of his goons.

"Hello gentleman. I've already removed the disturbance from my home, but thanks for coming by," I said, opening the door halfway.

"Malcolm Fitzgerald?" one of the officers questioned as he stopped me from closing the door.

"Yes."

"We have a warrant for your arrest," the taller of the two announced as he flashed his badge with a piece of paper.

"For what? I've never done anything illegal in my life. You must have the wrong guy."

"Everyone feels that way, Mr. Fitzgerald. You can speak your peace at the station," he replied.

"Officer, I'm not a criminal. I'm a law abiding citizen."

"I'm sure you are, but you're gonna have to come with us," the taller one stated.

"But I've done nothing wrong." I tried to pull away from him as he tried to contain me.

At that moment, he became a little more forceful as the

shorter officer came over to assist.

"But Officer, I can't go to jail. My wife and daughter need me right now. What could I have possibly done? I've done nothing illegal," I pleaded.

"I would say that money laundering and tax evasion is illegal, Mr. Fitzgerald, so you're under arrest," the taller officer announced. "You have the right to remain silent…"

As the shorter officer read me my rights, my life flashed before my eyes. How did this happen? Everything in my life was going so wrong and there was nothing I could do about it. I needed my wife. I needed to know that my daughter was okay. Thinking of the two people that mattered most, a single tear escaped my right eye as I was handcuffed.

"I need to call my lawyer. Don't I get to make a phone call?"

"Sir, you will be allowed a phone call at the station," the shorter officer advised.

I was so humiliated as the two men escorted me out of my building. Not only was the doorman in awe as he watched me get ushered into the police cruiser, all of my neighbors stared in disbelief, as the paparazzi snapped one picture after the next. Frustration and terror filled my mind. My emotions were going haywire when suddenly a lightbulb went off.

God works in mysterious ways was all I could think of when the cruiser finally pulled off. The more I thought about it, going to jail wouldn't be so bad after all. At least Sonny couldn't get to me in there. Time hadn't been on my side until now. Once my father-in-law's accounts were available in a couple of weeks I would be able to pay off Sonny and my life could go back to normal.

As soon as all of my Sonny drama was resolved, I was going to make sure I took my wife and daughter on a well needed vacation. It was imperative that I showed my wife how much I appreciated her. Charlotte was my rock. The sad part was that I had to go through so many women and so much drama before realizing what was right in front of me all along. My wife and daughter were all I needed. If that bitch Kennedi was really pregnant, too bad. If Cherry's son was really mine, tough shit. All that mattered to me at this moment was Charlotte and Gianni. I was going to spend the rest of my life proving my love to them. Breaking from my daze, I thought I would try and get one of the officers to call Charlotte from their cell phone. It was a long shot, but I'd been known to work my magic in impossible situations.

"Officer, is there any way you could call my wife? I need to let her know what is going on."

"Mr. Fitzgerald, we've told you before that you'll be given an opportunity to make a phone call once we get to the station," the shorter officer said in a heavy New York accent.

I could tell he was annoyed as he turned up the radio. I hated classical music. It made me feel like I was a part of some type of horror film. Irritated by the loud dramatic instruments, I could no longer contain myself.

"Sir, do you mind changing the station?"

"Mr. Fitzgerald, you're no longer important, and I'm not your personal DJ." Ignoring my request, he turned up the music even louder. Right when I thought he was done, he spoke again. So, how's Charlotte doing anyway?"

I was completely puzzled. "How do you know my wife's name?" Before he could respond, it was at that moment when I looked out of the window and noticed that we were going in the opposite direction of the police station.

"Officer, where are we going? This is not the way to the station."

"Malcolm, relax. It will all be over shortly."

"What will be over?"

"Your life."

Kennedi-24

My mind drifted off as I wondered what the hell I was going to do now that I was pregnant with Malcolm's child and he wanted nothing to do with me. Everything that had ever gone wrong in my life had Kasey's name written all over it and she was destined to pay. There was no way she was gonna get away with this.

How could I just lose everything I've ever wanted in the blink of an eye? Not only with Malcolm, but also with my career as a reality star. I didn't know how I was gonna make it. Something had to give.

Turning up the radio, I listened to Usher's song, *Climax*, while thinking about the last time Malcolm and I made love. The thought of Kasey having sex with Malcolm pained me. All of our lives she envied me and lived everyday to demise a plan on how to destroy me. Turning up the radio, I tried to stay focused just before my song was interrupted by a newsbreak.

Breaking News, hip-hop mogul Malcolm Fitzgerald was just arrested at his downtown penthouse. Charges have yet to be announced. Stay tuned as we update you with more details.

I immediately wondered what the hell was going on. "I just left there."

Reaching into my Celine handbag, I shuffled around until I found my cell phone. I wanted to give Malcolm a call to see if the radio report was true, but his phone went straight to voicemail. I was a nervous wreck. So badly I wanted to turn around to go check on my man, but he had to wait. It was now or never to get my revenge on Kasey.

As we approached the upscale neighborhoods of Beverly Hills, I wondered where the hell my sister was on her way to. My gas tank was on E, but I was determined not to lose my trail on her ass. Minutes later, we finally came to a stop on the north side of Sunset Boulevard. Staring in disbelief, I couldn't believe my eyes.

The grey stone Tudor mansion was gorgeous, and very similar to the one we'd filmed the reality show in. *Who the hell lives here,* I thought, looking at the beautiful water fountain in the front yard. Knowing Kasey, she was probably hooked up with some old, rich white man, funding her L.A. ride. Then again, since her fake ass loved kids so much, maybe she was a nanny to some rich actress. *This could be your only shot Kennedi at revenge, make it count*, I said to myself as my hazel eyes stared back at me in the mirror. Today that tramp Kasey was gonna pay. She would never get the chance to betray me again.

After pulling into a parking space on the street right in front of the beautiful mansion, I tucked my gun at my waist and quietly got out of the car. Being as incognito as possible, I made it into the gate unnoticed as Kasey pulled up the driveway. Hiding behind a rose bush, as soon as I shooed away a bumblebee, I lost Kasey.

"Where the hell did she go that fast," I whispered while making my way closer to the house.

The closer I got, I could hear voices that seemed to come from the backyard, so I made my way in that direction. Whoever lived in the house had to be loaded because there was a miniature waterpark with water slides and everything back there. This was any child's dream.

Ducking behind another set of rose bushes, I could hear the laughter of children playing in a pool house that was located a few feet away from the pool. To the right of me was the back of the huge estate. Even though I was taking a chance by trespassing on someone else's property, and really didn't know exactly where she was, I decided to go to the pool house and look for Kasey anyway. The closer I got, the voices were more profound and familiar. Drawing my gun, I didn't hesitate to kick the door open like I was on the fucking SWAT team.

As screams immediately shot across the room, I got the surprise of my life. Kasey was nowhere to be found. It was C.O. Bates, Sharrod's aunt and the bitch who made my life a living nightmare the entire two years I was in prison. She was obviously caring for Chase, China, and Kasey's son, Rashad.

"Bitch, put your hands where I can see them. Do what I said, Bates!" I ordered.

"Okay, okay," she said, placing her hands on her head. "Don't do anything crazy."

The fear in the children's eyes made me feel bad for a quick second, but I was out for blood. There was no time to get soft now. I had a job to do.

"Kennedi, why do you have a gun?" Chase asked afraid. He balled up and started to rock back and forth on the floor.

I ignored my son. There was no way I would allow him to take me off focus. "China, where is Kasey?"

Rolling her eyes not phased at all she spat, "I don't know, what's going on?"

"I'm here to take you both away from them," I advised her.

"I'm not going anywhere with you," China shot back.

"Sharrod will kill you first, Kennedi. He's not going to allow you to have those kids. You ain't want them all this time, so why now? Is it because you see Sharrod back on his feet getting money? You think you gonna live up in this mansion. This is Kasey's palace now. You gave Sharrod the green light to replace you when you betrayed him," C.O. Bates added.

"Bitch, shut up. You don't know shit about my life. Fuck, Kasey!"

"Why are you so jealous of that girl? She has been nothing but great to your children. If it wasn't for her, these kids would be lost. You didn't want nothing to do with them after you were released from prison, that's why my nephew hates you even more."

"You got me fucked up if you think I would ever be jealous of that slut. She wants to be me."

"That girl sacrificed the last couple of years for you," C.O. Bates continued.

"Did you just say sacrificed? You have no idea what I've lost because of the lengths I've gone through for Kasey. Just mind your business! Kasey is some shit and you stupid for thinking that bitch is such a great person."

"Kennedi, don't say that about Mommy Kasey. That's Daddy's wife."

My heart sunk. How could Sharrod do this? How could he have my son call Kasey, Mommy? I was hurt. Was this karma? Maybe everyone was right. Maybe I should've gotten out of jail and took care of my kids instead of chasing a dead end dream.

There was no telling where Kasey or Sharrod was and time was ticking. I had to think fast. Still holding my gun to C.O. Bates, I skimmed the room and saw a jump rope.

"Chase, bring Mommy the rope," I instructed.

"Kennedi, I'm scared. Are you gonna shoot me?" he asked.

Tears ran down my face. For once in my life I was sorry for not giving Chase what I wanted all my life, a mother. Was I as bad as the lady I despised more than anything in the world?

"Baby, I promise, I would never hurt you. Now, bring me the rope," I said, trying to hold it all together. Glancing over at C.O. Bates with her hands still in the air, I spit in her face.

"You nasty whore," Bates said, wiping her face with the back of her hand.

"I've been called worse, that's for you plotting on me in jail. Hands back up, Bates," I demanded. "Where's Sharrod now when you need him? Now, get in the chair," I ordered.

As I tied her up with the rope so she wouldn't get in my way, it was time to deal with the kids.

"My nephew will never allow you to get away with this. You have no respect," she continued to talk shit.

"Respect is earned. Just because you old don't mean you warrant me giving you an ounce of respect. Kick rocks, bitch."

"Your days are numbered," she said, shaking her head in disgust.

At that moment, I diverted my attention back to the kids that were in the corner shaking like fall leaves on a tree.

"Now, I need you to do me a favor, guys. I'm gonna put you in this closet…"

"No Kennedi, I don't want to go into the closet," Chase cried.

"I promise you that I'm coming back. It's just so you all can't get hurt."

"Me too," Kasey's son, Rashad questioned.

I nodded my head. "Yes, you too, Rashad," I lied. That little faggot was a part of Kasey and Sharrod. They were my enemies and he was on his own.

"I'm not getting in no closet," China's smartass objected.

"You're gonna do what I say, China. I'm your mother and you're going to listen to me. It's for your own good." I tried to stay calm.

"You're nothing to me!" China yelled as she tried to escape out the door.

Raising my gun at her, I saw a flash of Harry. Closing my eyes, I put my finger on the trigger. The horrible memories of Harry could all be erased that easy. No longer would I have to look at her face. She would be a constant reminder of Harry if I let her live.

"You better not, Kennedi!" C.O. Bates yelled.

"Kennedi, nooooo!" Chase followed, right before reality

set in. Opening my eyes and watching her turn around and look at me with so much fear made me realize she belonged to me. What was I thinking?

At the end of the day, she was my child, so I would have to learn to love her.

"China, please come back here," I said, putting my gun down at my waist.

As she walked back towards me with a look of complete fright in her eyes, I felt horrible. Reaching out to her, I cried. However, as I tried to hug her, she pulled away. I grabbed her as she fought me back.

"I hate you, Kennedi! I hate you!"

Tears flooded my face as I watched my broken daughter cry. I had to make things right, but for now it was my duty to teach Kasey and Sharrod a lesson for thinking I was a joke.

Ushering the kids into the double door toy closet, I closed the door while they wailed. Looking around the room, surprisingly, there was a chain along with a padlock lying a few feet away. I had no idea what it was for, but couldn't be more perfect to assist me. Picking up both items, I placed the chain through the two handles and then secured it with the lock. After making sure they couldn't escape, I turned around ready for war.

"Don't do this!" Bates yelled again, even though I ignored her.

Just as I walked out of the pool house, I was faced with my enemy. She looked like me more than ever, which made my flesh crawl. Kasey had changed from her freakum dress she used to seduce Malcolm into a pair of leggings and a *I Love My Hubby* tee on. The shirt had my nerves on fire. Thinking back to the ring on her finger, and Chase saying that she was, 'Daddy's Wife', I couldn't believe those two were married.

There was no need for me to hide anymore. As soon as she looked up, my presence stopped her right in her tracks. You would've thought she'd seen a ghost as she stood paralyzed with shock.

"What are you doing at my home? My husband would kill you if he knew you were here."

Before Kasey could say another word, I struck her across her temple as hard as I could with my gun. She was out cold. Now, it was time to formulate a plan to see what Sharrod was up to. One thing I learned from Kasey was being a twin had its advantages, especially for times like this. The twin switch plan was in full effect and it was my turn to give Kasey a taste of her own medicine. Sharrod would never know the difference. Switching our clothing made me sick, but it had to be done.

Now, I was out for blood and Kasey and Sharrod were gonna pay.

Malcolm-25

"What do you guys want from me?"

Turning up the classical music, the guys ignored me as they started driving faster than before as if they were in a hurry. The bumpy ride made my stomach do flips. My heart dropped. How could I be so stupid to fall for these imposters? With all of the people that witnessed me get in the police cruiser outside of my penthouse I could've possibly gotten away. With all that was on my mind, I wasn't focused. It was if I was awaiting my demise. The strong New York accent should've been a dead giveaway. Who the hell were these guys? My mind raced with confusion.

When the classical music stopped all of a sudden, Charlotte and Gianni's voices echoed through the speakers.

Malcolm, help us please! Why are these people doing this? They're gonna kill us, Malcolm. Please get in touch with the lawyers to see if they can rush the closure of my dad's estate. Oh my God, I'm afraid. Please give these people their money!

"*I want my Daddy!*" *Gianni cried.*

"*Go ahead baby, the nice man is gonna let you leave your daddy a message,*" *Charlotte calmed Gianni.*

"*Daddy, I want to come home. My wrists hurt really bad, Daddy. I don't like this game. I miss you. I just…*"

Before Gianni could finish, all of a sudden she let out a loud howl. As I listened to both Charlotte and Gianni being tortured and brutalized on a recording, I lost it.

"What the hell are you trying to prove? Where's my family?"

"Is that music better?" one of them joked.

"Guess you're not getting that phone call at the station after all," the other mobster instigated as they both burst into laughter.

"What have you all done with my family? Where's my daughter? Please answer me!" I begged.

Sonny must've gotten to my wife and daughter at the airport. I knew I shouldn't have listened to Charlotte when she denied security. When anger filled my body, I suddenly started to kick the windows. I wanted out. If they were gonna ignore me, I knew how to get their attention. I needed to know where my family was.

"What the hell is wrong with you? Calm your ass down," the shorter guy called out.

"Where's my family? If you don't tell me, you're gonna deal with me kicking this window until I tear it out the frame, got dammit!" I belted.

"That's all right. I'll fix his ass," the taller one said as he pulled over on the side of the secluded road. There wasn't another car in sight As soon as he opened the back door my foot went straight to his face.

"You dumb fuck!" he yelled as he grabbed me by my shirt.

I pounded him with my handcuffed hands trying to fight for my life, while the shorter guy grabbed me from behind. As soon as he hit me over the head with his gun, I was out cold.

When I finally came to, I was confused and I wondered where the hell I was. As I peered out of the window, all I could see were trees and open road. My head ached and my chest pounded. I didn't know what to do. Helplessness and defeat were the emotions that consumed me as I tried to adjust my wrists within the tight, uncomfortable cuffs. I just wanted answers.

As I sweated profusely, a vision of a familiar face appeared next to me in the backseat.

"Ma, is that you?" I asked rubbing my eyes.

"Malcolm, what have you gotten yourself into now?"

"Ma, what are you doing here?"

"Malcolm, I know I wasn't the best mother, but I thought that you would've learned from my mistakes. Son, I wanted you to grow up to be better than your father, to be better than me. How did you allow yourself to be caught up with these kind of people? They are gutter."

"But Ma, all I've tried to do was keep my nose clean and hustle to make a living; to take care of my family. That's all I wanted was to let them live comfortably and enjoy life."

"Boy, who are you fooling? You did all this for you. You like the flash and the fame. That's what drives you. It's nothing wrong with wanting fame, but when it is at the cost of your family, is when it's a problem. Look at how you've hurt Charlotte. How you've treated your wife is what you've taught my granddaughter about marriage. You've taught Gianni that it's okay for a man to love her and anyone else he chooses."

"That wasn't my intentions, Ma. I love my wife. I love Gianni. I never wanted to see them hurt."

"Your addiction to the limelight has caused them to be subjected to this violence. Look at what your father subjected me to. The fast life, got me hooked on drugs and caused me to contract AIDS. It caused me to be taken away from you and your sister."

"And I hate him for it!" I yelled.

"Well, hate yourself Malcolm, because you have turned into the womanizer that he was. You have become him."

"No, I haven't. I love my family. I'm gonna make things

right," I assured her.

"Malcolm, it's too late. You are about to…"

"Ma! Ma!" I yelled before she disappeared right before my eyes. What was happening? I was hallucinating and had no control over my emotions. As I rubbed my eyes trying to refocus and wipe the sweat from my brow, reality set in again. I was still in the back of the cruiser with the same two idiots.

"Where are we going? I just want to know my family is okay," I said, out of breath and exhausted. It felt as if my ribs were broken.

"You'll be reunited with them soon, Malcolm. You just have to be patient. Now, I don't know if you'll be joined together the way you'd like, but most definitely you will be together soon," the taller goon informed.

My heart raced as I closed my eyes wishing this were all a nightmare.

"What have you maggots done with my family?" I yelled again.

Suddenly, one of the goons' phone rang.

"Ahh, looks like you got a phone call, Malcolm," the shorter guy informed me in a sarcastic tone.

Lumps instantly started to form in my throat, as I feared the conversation that was about to take place.

"Malcolm, how's it going?" Sonny questioned.

"Sonny, why? Why are you torturing me this way? You know this wasn't really my fault. Why are you holding me accountable for something Frankie did? I kept my word and never told a soul about what happened? Why couldn't you just cut me a break?"

"Malcolm, has anyone ever told you that you talk too much?"

"Sonny, why? I just want to know why?"

"Malcolm, I don't know what to tell you. I guess you just chose the wrong friend in college. It's a shame that my nephew Frankie got you all caught up in his mess, but you should've known that I meant business years ago."

"Where's my family?" I questioned.

"They're very close by."

"So, where are your guys taking me?"

"Look, Malcolm quit your bitching and stop asking me all these questions. I gave you two years to pay me and you chose otherwise."

"How could I give you what I don't have?"

"Your wife informed me that two years ago she bailed you out of a similar situation, so it's obvious that you had the money, but just failed to pay your fucking debt. Guess you didn't consider me as a priority!" he yelled.

"Of course you were. But I do have a family to take care of, so I was just trying to flip the money that's all, Sonny. I'm sorry."

"Awe Malcolm, it's too late for sorries. You fucked up."

"I know, just give me another chance," I desperately pleaded.

"Your chances are up. I can't take another minute of your whining," Sonny responded. "Gentleman, have you arrived to the destination yet?"

As we pulled into a gas station on a secluded dirt road, I was puzzled. There wasn't one person in sight. As I stared out of the window, I wondered why Gianni and Charlotte weren't here. Maybe they were gonna let them go now that they had me.

Suddenly, both of the mobsters got out of the car with the phone. They were still talking to Sonny as I waited to see what was gonna happen next. Once they were finished talking, they threw the phone back into the car as Sonny continue to torment me. Watching them walk into the closed station, I wondered frantically what they were doing.

"Malcolm, you still there?" Sonny asked.

I responded with a weak, "Yes."

"So, Malcolm, help me understand. What possessed you to cheat on Charlotte with that gutter, poor, white trash Cherry?

She's a piece of work."

"I don't have an answer for that. All I can say is that I regret all I ever did to Charlotte everyday, and I regret not paying you as well."

"I'm sure you do," he responded in a matter of fact tone.

"Yes, Sonny. I'm sorry. I'm sorry for everything. Could you just give me a few more weeks? I'll make sure you get my wife's entire inheritance if you just let us live."

"Well, Malcolm it's a little too late. I feel bad that I had to involve that lovely Charlotte and Gianni in your shenanigans, but I couldn't let them live."

"Oh my God! Where are they?" I looked around praying that my daughter would come running out of the station and Sonny would give me a second chance.

"They're in the trunk of the cruiser. They're dead."

Instantly, my heart dropped and my emotions ran wild. Was this really happening? I couldn't believe that my family had been killed because of me. How could Sonny order death on my sweet child? There was no reason for me to live anymore.

"I didn't get a chance to get my hands on your mistress Ashley yet, but my enforcer Sharrod assured me he'd take care of her," Sonny added.

"Fuck her. All I care about is my family. Tell me you're lying, Sonny. Tell me that they're safe. I know you wouldn't do that to an innocent child."

"Actually I would if that child's father didn't hold up his end of the fucking deal. Charlotte, Gianni, Malcolm Jr., and that whore Cherry. Cherry actually sucked me off before we laid her to rest. They're all right behind you in the trunk."

"Noooooo. Why Sonny? What happened to no women, no kids?"

Sonny let out a loud roar of laughter. "Malcolm, you've been watching to many mob movies. Did you forget what I did to my lovely wife, Pam?" He laughed again. "Now, I've gotta go. It's time for you to meet your maker."

Before I could have another chance to plead my case, the phone went dead. Moments later, the smell of gasoline got stronger. Quickly turning around, I watched as one of the mobsters took off his fake uniform shirt and stuffed it into the gas tank. As the smell got stronger, I noticed the other guy pouring gasoline all over the car. Watching the gasoline stream down the windows and windshield, I felt helpless. If only I could get my family out of the trunk. Maybe they are still alive. As I kicked the window with what little fight I had left in me, the mobsters laughed.

"He really thinks he's getting outta there. Jimmy you got the lighter?" the shorter goon asked.

As sweat poured down my face, my heart raced. My body was filled with both fear and anger. There was no reason to live anymore without my family. All of my life I'd dodged many difficult situations. But this one was beyond my control and there was nothing I could do to help myself, nor my family. All because of me, my wife and my daughter were gone. I was never a spiritual person, but I felt it was necessary to have a heart to heart with my God. As I approached my demise, I watched the mobster flick the lighter as I closed my eyes and said a silent prayer.

Father God, I come to you with a humble heart. I ask that you forgive me for all my sins. I've made a lot of mistakes in my life, but you know my heart. I pray that you take me and my family to your kingdom and give us everlasting life.

Amen.

Kennedi-26

Walking into the mansion, I instantly felt ill. I had to ask myself over and over how the hell Sharrod was able to live like this, while staring at the portraits of him and Kasey all over the foyer. What made matters worse, was the portrait of Kasey and all three of the children. The way her ass smiled like they were one big happy family made my blood boil. She was living my life. It wasn't fair and Kasey and Sharrod were living life as if they were the royal family. I was there for the struggle when he was coming up and now she get's to reap the benefits, not on my watch.

"Who dat?" Sharrod's ignorant ass called out.

"It's me." I changed my voice to try and sound like Kasey.

"I thought you were taking a late evening swim with the kids?" Sharrod asked as I walked into the kitchen. Once we were face to face, my heart dropped. Pain and revenge filled my mind. "You okay, Kase? It looks like you just seen a ghost." He placed his hand on my shoulder as I stood paralyzed.

"Oh, I just don't feel good."

"Your morning sickness starting up again."

Morning sickness, I thought. "Umm…yeah, I guess so."

"Let me get you a ginger ale, baby. I can't wait til you get past your first trimester," Sharrod said in a sweet voice.

I couldn't believe Kasey was pregnant. No matter how much I tried to fight my feelings for Sharrod and fake like I didn't care about him marrying Kasey, it actually hurt down to the core. My heart was in pain and my stomach turned at the idea of Kasey carrying the baby of the man that I loved once upon of time.

As I rubbed my own stomach, I made sure my gun was tucked in the side of my leggings. The way he sashayed through the kitchen catering to me pissed me off. He never treated me like this as Kennedi.

As I sat in the sunroom and faked as if the television interested me, Sharrod brought me my glass of ginger ale. He was different. Sharrod even looked different. He was still big, but had lost a lot of weight. He was so gentle and acted like he was in love. He was never that way with me.

"So, baby, you never told me where you were all day. I know you weren't out watching that bitch, Kennedi again."

I had to bite my lip to keep from blowing my cover. Referencing me as a bitch was not cool. Getting back into character, I answered him in that whiny voice of Kasey's, "No, I went to the mall."

All the time I thought Sharrod put Kasey up to seducing Malcolm, but she'd obviously fucked him because she wanted to. The harder I tried to maintain my composure and not get upset, the angrier I got. It was obvious Sharrod wasn't aware that his precious wife was out and about scheming, fucking my man today.

"Alright. I told you I don't want my boss to accidently think you're Kennedi and kill you by mistake, so you gotta lay low," he continued.

"Please, I've got better things to do than stalk Kennedi all day."

"Man, wait 'til she find out we married," he chuckled. "That bitch is gonna be sick. You know she's been jealous of you since back in the day," Sharrod called out from the kitchen with a loud roar of laughter. "But I gotta plan for her ass."

"I know that's right, babe," I said, trying to hold back

my emotions.

"I told you to be patient and I was gonna take care of you, didn't I. See, that's why I always fucked with you. You did what you were told while your bitch ass sister had too much mouth."

As I watched the television waiting for the right time to attack Sharrod's ass, his phone rang. Some things never changed. It always irritated me how he took his calls on speakerphone.

You have a collect call from, Shawn Bunn, an inmate at Chowchilla Correctional Facility. To accept this call press 5.

Anger and animosity immediately ran through my veins. Why the hell was Shawn calling Sharrod?

"What's up, homey?" Sharrod answered.

"Actually, I'm feeling like shit. I've been calling Ray and Isis constantly, but they're not answering my calls. Somebody told me Ray might've gone to Jamaica for a while, but my own sister not answering my calls is a problem. Isis knows better. I'm worried sick. I would die if something ever happened to her," Shawn informed.

"Did you call the club?" Sharrod questioned.

"Yeah, and nobody has seen them. I spoke to one of the girls, Ginger who dances over there, and she said the last time she saw Isis was when they went out to a club a few weeks ago with that bitch, Kennedi." Shawn paused for a second. "I'm telling you, Sharrod. If Kennedi did anything to my sister, it's gonna be a fucking problem. One of my homies will smoke her ass."

"Not if I get to her first," Sharrod responded.

"Then I called you last week and you ain't answer. What's the deal?"

"Shawn, you know you my home girl, so stop trippin'. I've just been busy tryna help boss wrap up that project we been workin' on." It was obvious he was talking in code.

"Well, you need to tell him to hook me up and get me

out like he hooked you up."

"Be patient, it's all in the works. I told you that you were good," Sharrod assured.

"Man, I'm tired of this place, especially with Bates gone. She let me get away with everything. Where she at anyway?" Shawn asked.

"Down at the pool house with the kids. With Kasey pregnant I needed her to be here to help out with the kids. Plus, she only applied for the job at Chowchilla just to watch, Kennedi."

"True…true. So, where wifey at anyway?" Shawn inquired.

"In the sunroom, sick. Stop asking 'bout my wife, too."

"Sharrod, cut it out. I only fucked Kennedi because you made me," Shawn replied.

"The entire time I was locked up, I wondered what I could do to make that bitch pay for ratting me out. Yeah, I was mad about her fucking Q, but I got over it. Shit, me and Kasey was fucking the whole time I was with her. But that snitch shit was unacceptable."

"Yeah, you right."

"Thanks again for your help," Sharrod praised.

"No problem. I'm glad your aunt approached me with the idea. I was bored before that."

As they both burst into laughter, a single tear escaped my right eye. Listening to them laugh at me was truly gut wrenching. Not to mention, learning that my relationship with Shawn was all premeditated, hurt even more. The last two years with Shawn had all been a lie, and I'd fell for it. All my life I'd never trusted anyone. Just when I let my guard down, someone else proved me right to never trust again. My heart was broken with the amount of betrayal that I'd experienced throughout my life.

When Shawn's time was finally up and her call was disconnected, you could almost see steam coming from my ears.

Mad as hell, I made sure my gun was in an accessible place. Placing it right between the sofa's pillow cushions, I was ready to bust his ass as soon as I caught him slipping. One thing I knew about Sharrod, he kept guns all over the house, so I had to be smart. As I watched *E News,* Malcolm's picture appeared across the screen. Immediately, I turned the television up.

Hip Hop Mogul, Malcolm Fitzgerald along with his wife Charlotte and daughter Gianni Fitzgerald were reported missing today by his assistant Charles West. Earlier we reported that Malcolm was arrested for charges unknown. Well, after Mr. West made a couple of phone calls to see where Mr. Fitzgerald was being held, police informed him that they never ordered a warrant for Mr. Fitzgerald's arrest. No one has heard from Mr. Fitzgerald since he was taken away in handcuffs from his home hours ago. Police are looking for anyone who has any information on Mr. Fitzgerald and his family's whereabouts. Police are in search of both of Malcolm Fitzgerald's alleged mistresses for questioning, reality star Ashley Jacobs and video vixen, Cherry Stevens.

"Ha! Boss finally got that nigga! See, this is why I told you to stay away from Kennedi's ass!" Sharrod yelled with excitement.

Damn, I whispered under my breath. My heart ached wondering if Malcolm was alright. Lost into the TV, Sharrod startled me as he placed his hand on my shoulder. I didn't even realize he'd come back in the room.

"Shit, since the police are looking for Kennedi's ass, they better hope I don't see her first. Now that boss got her little boyfriend, I can kill her ass."

I had to speak up. "Why you gotta kill her? You must still love her."

"Please. I hate that bitch," Sharrod replied with a huge frown. "Awww. Are you gonna be upset if I kill your sister?" he teased before kissing me in my mouth.

All of a sudden my stomach started to turn and I threw

up all over him.

"Damn, Kase you got shit all over me!" he yelled. "Maria! Maria! Come clean this shit up, please."

Sharrod pulled off his shirt, which exposed the gun at his waist. Seconds later, a Hispanic older woman ran in.

"Oh, Senorita Jones, are you okay? You need me to help you to the bathroom. I run you bubble bath."

"No, thanks, Maria."

"You need to go lay down, Kasey. I'm about to call down to the pool house and have Auntie bring the kids in. It's dark outside. I don't know why she ain't brought them up here yet," Sharrod said.

"Babe let them be. They were having fun in the pool house. They're good."

"Maria, get Kasey some more ginger ale before you head out, please. I'm sorry, I know it's getting late."

"No problem, senor," she answered.

After Maria cleaned up my vomit, she then went back upstairs to get her things before she left for the day. Thank God. I would hate to have to kill her for no reason.

Sharrod pointed at me. "Take your shirt off, baby, you got vomit all over you."

"No, I'm okay," I answered. I didn't want him anywhere near me.

Just as Sharrod started to make his way back over to me, the front door flung open. It was Kasey.

"Sharrod, oh my God, it's Kennedi!" I quickly yelled.

Without hesitation, Sharrod instantly went into attack mode. Pulling a gun straight from his waist, he started firing straight at Kasey. It felt like a weight had been lifted as soon as I watched her body fall to the floor.

Now, it was my turn to bust off. Grabbing my gun from the seat cushion, adrenaline flushed through my veins. It was now or never.

"Is she dead?" I yelled from across the room.

Standing over Kasey, Sharrod shot one more bullet straight into her head.

"Now, she is."

It hurt to see that someone I'd spent half my life with wanted me dead that badly. In order for me to be able to walk this Earth freely, Sharrod had to go. As I raised my gun up at him, I crept up closer with a smile plastered across my face.

"Oh my God...Kasey! Oh my God!" Sharrod yelled as he lifted her hand.

The matching cross tattoos they shared was a sign that he'd killed the wrong person. By the time he turned around and faced me, my gun was pointed directly at him. I smiled.

"Sharrod, thank you so much for taking care of that for me. Guess you're good for something."

It looked as if he could spit fire. "You bitch. You fuckin' bitch."

"I can be all the bitches in the world, but your wife's a dead bitch," I responded. "Oh, by the way I guess she didn't tell you that I caught her in bed with Malcolm today."

"Shut up! You lyin'!"

"Oh, I'm not lying. How do you think I was able to follow her dumb ass here? How does it feel to kill your wife and baby at the same damn time?" I asked, getting a kick out of watching Sharrod so upset.

"Put the gun down, Kennedi," he ordered.

"No, you put your gun down. For the past two years you lived every day creating a plan to destroy my life. You never loved me. You were fucking my sister the entire time. After I kill you, I'm going to kill your fat ass Aunt and take my kids away from this place."

"You will never see my kids again bitch because you are gonna die tonight."

As he fired his gun at me and missed, the vase of roses behind me broke and glass shattered everywhere.

All hell broke loose as we fired shots at each other. We

were both out for blood and there was only gonna be one of us standing, or neither of us.

"I hate you! You made me kill my wife, and now you're gonna die!" Sharrod yelled, firing another shot my way as I jumped behind the couch. It hurt so bad that he chose Kasey over me.

"Sharrod, you've betrayed me all these years. Yeah, I fucked Q, but you fucked my sister, my blood! You had a child with her! You were wrong, Sharrod, and you want me dead so bad. I hate you! I hate you, Sharrod!" I cried.

No longer did I care about shielding myself, I was angry. I came out from behind the couch and continued to empty my gun as I hit Sharrod in his upper body as he collapsed. The anger that filled my body made me numb. As I grabbed my chest and looked at my hand filled with blood, I realized I was hit. As blood gushed from my chest, I started to feel faint I could no longer keep my eyes open.

TO BE CONTINUED…
THE SEQUEL, A-LIST...COMING SOON.

ALSO BY

Miss KP

Check out these and other titles at:
www.lifechangingbooks.net

ORDER FORM

MAIL TO:
PO Box 423
Brandywine, MD 20613
301-362-6508

FAX TO:
301-579-9913

Ship to:

Address:

Date: Phone:

City & State: Zip:

Email:

Make all money orders and cashiers checks payable to: **Life Changing Books**

Qty.	ISBN	Title	Release Date	Price
	0-9741394-2-4	Bruised by Azarel	Jul-05	$ 15.00
	0-9741394-7-5	Bruised 2: The Ultimate Revenge by Azarel	Oct-06	$ 15.00
	0-9741394-3-2	Secrets of a Housewife by J. Tremble	Feb-06	$ 15.00
	0-9741394-6-7	The Millionaire Mistress by Tiphani	Nov-06	$ 15.00
	1-934230-99-5	More Secrets More Lies by J. Tremble	Feb-07	$ 15.00
	1-934230-95-2	A Private Affair by Mike Warren	May-07	$ 15.00
	1-934230-96-0	Flexin & Sexin Volume 1	Jun-07	$ 15.00
	1-934230-89-8	Still a Mistress by Tiphani	Nov-07	$ 15.00
	1-934230-91-X	Daddy's House by Azarel	Nov-07	$ 15.00
	1-934230-88-X	Naughty Little Angel by J. Tremble	Feb-08	$ 15.00
	1-934230820	Rich Girls by Kendall Banks	Oct-08	$ 15.00
	1-934230839	Expensive Taste by Tiphani	Nov-08	$ 15.00
	1-934230782	Brooklyn Brothel by C. Stecko	Jan-09	$ 15.00
	1-934230669	Good Girl Gone bad by Danette Majette	Mar-09	$ 15.00
	1-934230804	From Hood to Hollywood by Sasha Raye	Mar-09	$ 15.00
	1-934230707	Sweet Swagger by Mike Warren	Jun-09	$ 15.00
	1-934230677	Carbon Copy by Azarel	Jul-09	$ 15.00
	1-934230723	Millionaire Mistress 3 by Tiphani	Nov-09	$ 15.00
	1-934230715	A Woman Scorned by Ericka Williams	Nov-09	$ 15.00
	1-934230685	My Man Her Son by J. Tremble	Feb-10	$ 15.00
	1-924230731	Love Heist by Jackie D.	Mar-10	$ 15.00
	1-934230812	Flexin & Sexin Volume 2	Apr-10	$ 15.00
	1-934230748	The Dirty Divorce by Miss KP	May-10	$ 15.00
	1-934230758	Chedda Boyz by CJ Hudson	Jul-10	$ 15.00
	1-934230766	Snitch by VegasClarke	Oct-10	$ 15.00
	1-934230693	Money Maker by Tonya Ridley	Oct-10	$ 15.00
	1-934230774	The Dirty Divorce Part 2 by Miss KP	Nov-10	$ 15.00
	1-934230170	The Available Wife by Carla Pennington	Jan-11	$ 15.00
	1-934230774	One Night Stand by Kendall Banks	Feb-11	$ 15.00
	1-934230278	Bitter by Danette Majette	Feb-11	$ 15.00
	1-934230299	Married to a Balla by Jackie D.	May-11	$ 15.00
	1-934230308	The Dirty Divorce Part 3 by Miss KP	Jun-11	$ 15.00
	1-934230316	Next Door Nympho By CJ Hudson	Jun-11	$ 15.00
	1-934230286	Bedroom Gangsta by J. Tremble	Sep-11	$ 15.00
	1-934230340	Another One Night Stand by Kendall Banks	Oct-11	$ 15.00
	1-934230359	The Available Wife Part 2 by Carla Pennington	Nov-11	$ 15.00
	1-934230332	Wealthy & Wicked by Chris Renee	Jan-12	$ 15.00
	1-934230375	Life After a Balla by Jackie D.	Mar-12	$ 15.00
	1-934230251	V.I.P. by Azarel	Apr-12	$ 15.00
	1-934230383	Welfare Grind by Kendall Banks	May-12	$ 15.00

			Total for Books	$

Shipping Charges (add $4.95 for 1-4 books*) $

Total Enclosed (add lines) $

* Prison Orders- Please allow up to three (3) weeks for delivery.

Please Note: We are not held responsible for returned prison orders. Make sure the facility will receive books before ordering.

*Shipping and Handling of 5-10 books is $6.95, please contact us if your order is more than 10 books. (301)362-6508